MADEL...
shortlist...
won the...
Literary...
Simple R...
at the Perimeter, was ...
Literature Award and won the Frank... ...
LiBeraturpreis. Her books and stories have been translated into 23 languages, and her essays have appeared in *Granta*, the *Guardian*, the *Financial Times*, *Five Dials*, and *Brick*. Her story 'The Wedding Cake' was shortlisted for the 2015 *Sunday Times* EFG Short Story Award. The daughter of Malaysian-Chinese immigrants to Canada, she lives in Montreal.

'Madeleine Thien's powerful new novel reminds us [that] leaving the past behind is rarely simple ... Thien brilliantly evokes 1970s Cambodia, from the chaos of Phnom Penh to the sweltering, filthy work camps, from the interrogation centres to the lush forests. But she's equally adept at bringing cold, clean Montreal to life, from its icy streets to Hiroji's abandoned apartment... Her novel leaves the reader deeply moved and, ultimately, hopeful' *Irish Times*

'A nightmare account of the horrors of man's inhumanity to man and its damage to the psyche' *Daily Mail*

'This sensitive novel captures the emotions as well as the desperate history of Cambodia during the war and the Khmer Rouge horrors. Madeleine Thien uses her extraordinary talents to describe entanglements that stretch from Phnom Penh to Montreal, the pain intact, while somehow renewing our common humanity' Elizabeth Becker, author of *When the War Was Over*

'As a book that explores memory, loss and madness – both political and personal – *Dogs at the Perimeter* is extraordinarily good, incredibly haunting and compassionate' *Reading Matters*

'Madeleine Thien's extraordinary second novel offers an unflinching portrayal – at once intimate and profound – of the Cambodian genocide, and the long-lasting effects of history and violence on both our contemporary culture and everyday lives ... *Dogs at the Perimeter* firmly establishes Thien as one of Canada's strongest and most original voices' Johanna Skibsrud, author of *The Sentimentalists*

'A moving, densely poetic narrative which implicitly asks us to consider the essence of who we are, our personal connections and why they are precious' *Metro*

'An achingly beautiful novel about one of last century's most horrendous catastrophes ... *Dogs at the Perimeter* is a remarkably crafted book by an author who hasn't flinched from the challenge' *Canberra Times*

'While many books have been written about Cambodia's time under the Khmer Rouge, it is more difficult to find works of fiction which tackle this difficult subject ... a haunting and moving novel' *Asian Review of Books*

'Ms Thien's sparse, elegant writing gives *Dogs at the Perimeter* a beauty that is all the more poignant for its subject matter ... The strife in Indo-China has inspired some astonishing writing in recent decades, both fiction and non-fiction. *Dogs at the Perimeter* belongs with the best of such works. But it also tells a more universal story about being borne back into the past – and the inescapability of history' *Economist*

Madeleine Thien

Dogs
at the
Perimeter

❖

A NOVEL

GRANTA

This story is written with love for my Cambodian friends.

I am grateful to the Center for Neuroscience and Society at the University of Pennsylvania for scholarship assistance during my research.

Granta Publications, 12 Addison Avenue, London W11 4QR

First published in Great Britain by Granta Books 2012
Paperback edition published by Granta Books 2013
This edition published by Granta Books 2017
Originally published in Canada in 2011 by McClelland & Stewart, Toronto

Copyright © 2011 by Madeleine Thien

Madeleine Thien has asserted her moral right under the Copyright, Designs and Patents Act, 1988, to be identified as the author of this work.

McClelland & Stewart acknowledge the financial support of the Government of Canada through the Book Publishing Industry Development Program and that of the Government of Ontario through the Ontario Media Development Corporation's Ontario Book Initiative. McClelland & Stewart further acknowledge the support of the Canada Council for the Arts and the Ontario Arts Council for their publishing program.

The author wishes to thank the Conseil des arts et des lettres du Québec for its financial support.

The epigraph and the lines on page 79 are from Haing S. Ngor's *Survival in the Killing Fields*, written with Roger Warner. Every effort has been made to contact the copyright holder and the publisher will be happy to amend the credit line as necessary in subsequent printings.

Zasetsky excerpt reprinted by permission of the publisher from *The Man With a Shattered World: The History of a Brain Wound* by A.R. Luria, with a Foreword by Oliver Sacks, p. 86, Cambridge, Mass.: Harvard University Press, Copyright © 1972 by Michael Cole. Foreword copyright © 1987 by Oliver Sacks.

Words attributed to Vesna Vulovic on page 21 are from her interview with Philip Baum, printed in the April 2002 edition of *Aviation Security International*.

Chea's words on pages 107–108 and Prasith's words on page 108 are adapted from source material cited in Elizabeth Becker's exceptional *When the War Was Over: Cambodia and the Khmer Rouge Revolution* (Public Affairs, 1986).

Elie is inspired by the work and life of Vancouver artist Anne Adams. Further details can be found in "Unravelling Bolero: progressive aphasia, transmodal creativity and the right posterior neocortex" by William W. Seeley et al., published in *Brain* (2008), 131, 39–41.

An excerpt from this novel appeared in *Granta* 114.

A CIP catalogue record for this book is available from the British Library.

1 3 5 7 9 10 8 6 4 2

ISBN 978 1 84708 491 0

Typset in Van Dijck by M&S, Toronto
Offset by M Rules
Printed and bound by CPI Group (UK) Ltd, Croydon, CR0 4YY

MIX
Paper from
responsible sources
FSC® C020471

for my mother

Tell the gods what is happening to me.

HAING S. NGOR, *Survival in the Killing Fields*

Saturday, February 18
[fragment]

On November 29, 2005, my friend Dr. Hiroji Matsui walked out of Montreal's Brain Research Centre at 7:29 in the evening. On the security video, his expression gives nothing away. For a brief moment, the camera captures him in passing: greying hair, neatly combed. Silver-framed eyeglasses, intense brows, a stubborn chin, the softness of an old man's face. He wears no coat, despite the freezing temperatures, and he carries nothing, not even the briefcase with which he had arrived that morning. He exits through a side door, down a flight of metal steps. And then Hiroji walked into the city and disappeared into air. The officer assigned to Hiroji's case told me that, without evidence of foul play, there was very little the police could do. In this world of constant surveillance and high security, it is still remarkably easy to vanish. People go to great lengths to abandon their identities, holding no credit cards or bank cards, no insurance papers, pension plans, or driver's licences. I wanted to tell the officer what I believed, that Hiroji's disappearance was only temporary, but the words didn't come. Just as before, they didn't come to me in time. Many of the missing, the officer went on, no longer wish to be themselves, to be associated with their abandoned identity. They go to these great lengths in the hope that they will never be found.

[end]

Janie

❖

They sleep early and rise in the dark. It is winter now. The nights are long but outside, where the leaves have fallen from the branches, the snowed-in light comes through. There is a cat who finds the puddles of sunshine. She was small when the boy was small, but then she grew up and left him behind. Still, at night, she hunkers down on Kiri's bed, proprietorial. They were born just a few weeks apart, but now he is seven and she is forty-four. My son is the beginning, the middle, and the end. When he was a baby, I used to follow him on my hands and knees, the two of us crawling over the wood floors, the cat threading between our legs. *Hello, hello,* my son would say. *Hello, my good friend. How are you?* He trundled along, an elephant, a chariot, a glorious madman.

It is twilight now, mid-February. Sunday.

Tonight's freezing rain has left the branches crystalline. Our home is on the second floor, west facing, reached by a twisting staircase, the white paint chipping off, rust burnishing the edges. Through the window, I can see my son. Kiri puts a record on, he shuffles it gingerly out of its cardboard sleeve, holding it lightly between his fingertips. I know the one he always chooses. I know how he watches the needle lift and the mechanical arm move into place. I know the outside but not the quiet, not the way his thoughts rise up, always jostling, always various, not how they untangle from one another or how they fall so inevitably into place.

Kiri is in grade two. He has his father's dark-brown hair, he has startling, beautiful eyes, the same colour as my own. His name, in Khmer, means "mountain." I want to run up the stairs and turn my key in the lock, the door to my home swinging wide open.

When my fear outweighs my need – fear that Kiri will look out the window and see this familiar car, that my son will see me – I turn the ignition, steer myself from the sidewalk, and roll away down the empty street. In my head, ringing in my ears, the music persists, his body swaying like a bell to the melody. I remember him, crumpled on the floor, looking up at me, frightened. I try to cover this memory, to focus on the blurring lights, the icy pavement. My bed is not far away but a part of me wants to keep on driving, out of the city, down the high-way straight as a needle. Instead, I circle and circle the residential streets. A space opens up in front of Hiroji's apartment, where I have been sleeping these last few weeks, and I edge the car against the curb.

Tomorrow will come soon, I tell myself. Tomorrow I will see my son.

The wind swoops down, blowing free what little heat I have. I can barely lock the door and get upstairs fast enough. Inside, I pull off my boots but keep my coat and scarf on against the chill. Hiroji's cat, Taka the Old, skips ahead of me, down the long hallway. On the answering machine, the message light is flashing and I hit the square button so hard the machine hiccups twice before complying.

Navin's voice. "I saw the car," my husband says. "Janie? Are you there?" He waits. In the background, my son is calling out. Their voices seem to echo. "No, Kiri. Hurry up, kiddo. Back to bed." I hear footsteps, a door closing, and then Navin coming back. He says he wants to take Kiri to Vancouver for a few weeks, that the time, and distance, might help us. "We'll stay at Lena's place," he says. I am nodding, agreeing with every word – Lena's home has stood empty since she died last year – but a numb grief is flowing through me.

One last message follows. I hear a clicking on the line, then the beep of keys being pressed, once, twice, three times. The line goes dead.

The fridge is remarkably empty. I scan its gleaming insides, then do a quick inventory: old bread in the freezer and in the cupboard two cans of diced tomatoes, a tin of smoked mussels, and, heaven, three bottles of wine. I liberate the bread and the mussels, pour a glass of sparkling white, then stand at the counter until the toaster ejects my dinner. Gourmet. I peel back the lid of the can and eat the morsels one by one. The wine washes the bread down nicely. Everything is gone too soon but the bottle of wine that accompanies me to the sofa, where I turn the radio on. Music swells and dances through the apartment.

This bubbly wine is making me morose. I drink the bottle quickly in order to be rid of it. "Only bodies," Hiroji once told me, "have pain." He had been in my lab, watching me pull a motor neuron from Aplysia. Bodies, minds: to him they were the same, one could not be considered without the other.

Half past ten. It is too early to sleep but the dark makes me uneasy. I want to call Meng, my oldest friend, we have not spoken in more than two weeks, but it is the hour of the wolves in Paris. My limbs feel light and I trickle, wayward, through the rooms. On the far side of the apartment, in Hiroji's small office, the windows are open and the curtains seem to move fretfully, wilfully. The desk has exploded, maybe it happened last week, maybe earlier, but now all the papers and books have settled into a more balanced state of nature. Still, the desk seems treacherous. Heaped all over, like a glacier colonizing the surface, are the pages I have been working on. Taka the Old has been here: the paper is crumpled and still faintly warm.

Since he disappeared, nearly three months ago now,

I've had no contact with Hiroji. I'm trying to keep a record of the things he told me: the people he treated, the scientists he knew. This record fills sheet after sheet – one memory at a time, one place, one clue – so that every place and every thought won't come at once, all together, like a deafening noise. On Hiroji's desk is an old photograph showing him and his older brother standing apart, an emerald forest behind them. Hiroji, still a child, smiles wide. They wear no shoes, and Junichiro, or James, stands with one hand on his hip, chin lifted, challenging the camera. He has a bewitching, sad face.

Sometimes this apartment feels so crowded with loved ones, strangers, imagined people. They don't accuse me or call me to account, but I am unable to part with them. In the beginning, I had feared the worst, that Hiroji had taken his own life. But I tell myself that if this had been a suicide, he would have left a note, he would have left something behind. Hiroji knew what it was to have the missing live on, unending, within us. They grow so large, and we so empty, that even the coldest winter nights won't swallow them. I remember floating, a child on the sea, alone in the Gulf of Thailand. My brother is gone, but I am looking up at the white sky and I believe, somehow, that I can call him back. If only I am brave enough, or true enough. Countries, cities, families. Nothing need disappear. At Hiroji's desk, I work quickly. My son's voice is lodged in my head, but I have lost the ability to keep him safe. I know that no matter what I say, what I make, the things I have done can't be forgiven. My own hands seem to mock me, they tell me the further I go to escape, the greater the distance I must travel back. You should never have left the reservoir, you should have stayed in the caves. Look around, we ended up back in the same place, didn't we? The buildings across the street fall dark, yet the words keep coming, accumulating like snow, like dust, a fragile cover that blows away so easily.

Sunday, February 19
[fragment]

Elie was fifty-eight years old when she began to lose language. She told Hiroji that the first occurrence was in St. Michael's Church in Montreal, when the words of the Lord's Prayer, words she had known almost from the time she had learned to speak, failed to materialize on her lips. For a brief moment, while the congregation around her prayed, the whole notion of language diminished inside her mind. Instead, the priest's green robes struck her as infinitely complicated, the winter coats of the faithful shifted like a collage, a pointillist work, a Seurat: precision, definition, and a rending, rending beauty. The Lord's Prayer touched her in the same bodily way that the wind might, it was the sensation of sound but not meaning. She felt elevated and alone, near to God and yet cast out.

And then the moment passed. She came back and so did the words. A mild hallucination, Elie thought. *Champagne in the brain.*

She went home and did what she always did. She closed the glass doors of her studio, unlatched the windows, lifted them high, and she painted. It was winter so she wore her coat over two shirts and fleece sweatpants, thick socks, Chinese slippers on her feet, and a woollen hat on her head. A decade ago she had been a biomechanical engineer, researching motor control, lecturing at McGill University, but at the age of forty-six, she had abandoned that life. Now, experience unfolded in a different pitch and tone, it was more fluid, more transitory, it enclosed her like the battering sea under broken light. When she closed her eyes she saw how the corners of improbable things touched – a bird and a person and a pencil rolling off a child's table – entwined, and became the same substance. Even her loved ones seemed different, more contained and solid, like compositions, iterations in her head. Painting was everything. She painted until she couldn't feel her arms anymore, ten, twelve hours at a time, every single day, and even then it wasn't enough. She told her husband, Gregor, that it was as if she had arrived at high noon, the hour when all forces converge. Gregor, a chef, grew used to falling asleep to the rhythms of Debussy and Ravel and Fauré, Elie's preferred accompaniments. Her husband grew accustomed to the smell of oil paint on her skin, the way she gestured with her hands in place of words, the way she gazed out with a new-found passion and righteousness. "I can see," he heard her calling to him one day. "Look what I can see."

"I thought," Elie told Hiroji, when he had been treating her for many years, "that my entire past was fantasy. Only my present was real."

The champagne in the brain began reoccurring, blotting out people's names, song lyrics, street names, book titles. She felt sometimes as if the words themselves had vanished, in her thoughts, her speech, and even her handwriting. There was a stopper in her throat and a black hole in her mind. In her paintings, she turned music into images, the musical phrases playing out like words, the words breaking into geometric shapes, her paintings grasping all the broken, brilliant fragments. When she worked, there were no more barriers between herself and reality, the image could say everything that she could not. Increasingly, she could not speak much. But she could live with losing language, if that was the price. This seemed, back then, a small price.

She was painting when she noticed the tremors in her right arm.

The first time she had met Hiroji, he had asked her if she found speaking effortful. The word had seemed to her like the priest's green robe that day in St. Michael's

Church, an image blocking out all other ideas. Yes, how *effortful* it was. "I'm decaying," she told Hiroji, surprising even herself.

"What do you mean?" he asked her.

"I can't . . . with the . . ." She put her hands together, straining to find the words. "There's too much."

Hiroji sent her for diagnostic testing. Those MRI films are conclusive. The first thing that strikes the viewer is the white line, the fragile outline of the skull, surprisingly thin. And then, within the skull, the grey matter folded around the hub of white matter. What has happened is that her left brain, the dominant side (she is right-handed), has atrophied – it is wasting away in the same manner that a flower left too long in the vase withers. Throughout Elie's left brain this disintegration is happening. Language is only the first thing that she will lose. It may come to pass that, one day soon, she will not be able to move the entire right side of her body.

The images show something else too. While one side of her has begun to atrophy, the other side is burgeoning. Elie's right brain has been creating grey matter – neurons – and all that extra tissue is collecting in the back of her brain, in the places where visual images are processed.

"It's a kind of asymmetry," Hiroji had told her, "a kind of imbalance in your mind, between words and pictures."

"So what is it, all this, that I'm making? Where is it coming from?" She waved her hands at the bare walls, as if to pull her own paintings into the room, to trail them behind her like an army.

"It comes from the inner world," Hiroji said, "but isn't that where all painting comes from?"

"My diseased inner world," she said. "I'm at war. I'm dwindling, aren't I?" She picked up the MRI scans from his desk. "Do you paint, Doctor?"

He shook his head.

"Have you ever thought about it?"

"No."

"Why not?"

He paused for a moment. "My mother painted. She was a Buddhist, and she used to tell me that I was too analytical, that I had no understanding of the ephemeral side of things."

"The ephemeral," she said doubtfully. "Like dancing?"

He laughed. "Yes, like dancing."

Hiroji kept Elie under what is known as surveillance MR imaging. Scan after scan, year by year, the films show the imbalance widening. Three years after her diagnosis, Elie's paintings, too, began to change. Where once she had delighted in turning music into complex mathematical and abstract paintings, intense with colour and the representation of rhythm, now she painted precise cityscapes, detailed, almost photographic. "I see differently," she told him. "It comes to me less holy than before." He wanted her to go further, to explain this holiness, but she just shook her head and poured the tea, her right hand trembling.

"The conceptual and the abstract," Hiroji told her, "are no longer as accessible. Your interior world has changed."

Hiroji and I co-authored a paper on Elie's condition. He described to me how, in Elie's home, her paintings graced the walls. He had the sense that they pleased her because they brought the interior world into the world that we live in, the one that we hold and touch, that we see and smell. "Soon," she had told him, tapping her fingers against her chest, "there will be no inside."

Elie is almost completely mute now. When she telephoned Hiroji, she wouldn't speak. She would hit the keypad two or three times, making a kind of Morse code, before hanging up again. Her disease is degenerative, a quickening loss of neurons and glia in the other parts of her brain, impeding speech, movement, and finally breathing itself. Unable to paint, she and Gregor spend long days at the riverside, where, she once told Hiroji, things move, ephemeral, and nothing stays the same.

Two years ago, delivering a lecture in Montreal, Hiroji spoke briefly about consciousness. He said that he imagined the brain as a hundred billion pinballs, where the ringing of sound, in all its amplitude and velocity, contained every thought and impulse, all our desires spoken and unspoken, self-serving, survivalist, and contradictory. The number of possible brain states exceeds the number of elementary particles in the universe. Maybe what exists beneath (tissue and bone and cells) and what exists above (ourselves, memory, love) can be reconciled and understood as one thing, maybe it is all the same, the mind is the brain, the mind is the soul, the soul is the brain, etc. But it's like watching a hand cut open another hand, remove the skin, and examine the tissue and bone. All it wants is to understand itself. The hand might become self-aware, but won't it be limited still?

A few days after the lecture, Hiroji received a letter from a man recently diagnosed with Alzheimer's. *I have been wondering,* the man wrote, *how to measure what I will lose. How much circuitry, how many cells have to become damaged before I, before the person my children know, is gone? Is there a self buried in the amygdala or the hippocampus? Is there one burst of electricity that stays constant all my life? I would like to know which part of the mind remains untouched, barricaded, if there is any part of me that lasts, that is incorruptible, the absolute centre of who I am.*

[end]

Before, on my sleepless nights, I used to tiptoe down the hallway and stand in Kiri's open doorway. My son, collector and purveyor of small blankets, is a light snorer. The sound of his breaths calmed me. Daring to enter, I would listen to his sleep, to the funny, stuttering exhalations that seemed altogether unearthly. Kiri, you are a godsend, I'd think. A mystery.

Taka the Old appears at the ledge of the window. Hiroji's cat watches me nervously, twitchily. Hours ago, I must have forgotten to remove my coat so I unbutton it now, shake it off, and fold it neatly over the back of a chair. The cat sidles nearer. We are two nocturnal creatures, lost in thought, except that she is sober. She rubs her face against the coat's empty arms, she purrs into its dangling hood.

I open the curtains. Nearly four in the morning and the view outside is fairy-tale white, a sharpened landscape that seems to rebuke the darkness, *Go back, go back, return from whence you came!* Snowdrifts and frozen eaves merge into cars, outlined in inches of snow. On the frosted windowpanes, I trace Khmer letters, Khmer words, but mine is a child's uncertain calligraphy, too wide, too clumsy. I was eleven years old when I left Cambodia, and I have never gone back. Years ago, on the way to Malaysia with my husband, I glimpsed it from the air. Its beauty, unchanged, unremitting, opened a wound in me. I was seated at the window and the small plane was flying low. It was the rainy season and Cambodia was submerged, a drowned place, the flooded land a plateau of light. From above, there were no cars or scooters that

I could see, just boats plying the waterways, pursued by the ribbon of their slipstream.

Silence eats into every corner of the room, creeping over the furniture, over the cat. She paces the room like a zoo lion. At the desk, I sharpen pencils ferociously, lining them up in a row.

On the floor is the file I keep returning to. When Hiroji disappeared, I had found it sitting on his kitchen table and had taken it away, never mentioning it to anyone, not the police, not even Navin. I had kept it in an old suitcase, as if it were a memento, a relic that Hiroji asked me to safeguard. The file contains the same documents and maps, the same letters from James, that Hiroji asked me to examine last year. I remember him unfolding the map, putting his finger against Phnom Penh, *here*, where the ink is smudged, the city at the confluence of the rivers. Back then, the map had seemed too flimsy to me, too abstract, a drawing of a country that had little relation to the country I had left behind. I couldn't see what he was seeing.

James Matsui had vanished in 1975. Four years earlier, having finished his residency at St. Paul's Hospital in Vancouver, he had signed up with the International Red Cross. Soon after, he had left Canada and landed in Saigon, into the mayhem of the Vietnam War. That same year, Nixon's bombs were falling on Cambodia, spies were breaking into the Watergate building, scientists had found a way to splice DNA, but I was young and didn't know those stories. I was eight years old, a child in Phnom Penh, and the fighting, at that time, raged in the borderlands. I remember staring up at the sky, transfixed by the airplanes. They were everywhere above us – commercial planes, fighter planes, transport planes, helicopters – a swarm that never ceased. My father told me about a woman named Vesna Vulovic. The plane she was travelling in had exploded over Czechoslovakia and she had fallen thirty-three thousand feet to the ground. She had survived. I named all of my dolls – I had three – Vesna. To me, she was like a drop of rain or a very tiny bird, someone whom the gods had overlooked.

From the file, I remove James's letters to Hiroji. Born Junichiro Matsui, nicknamed Ichiro when he was a boy, he chose the name James when he was a teenager. His letters home are brief, scattered with ellipses, and yet I keep returning to them, convinced that I have missed some crucial detail. In 1972, the Red Cross sent him up the Mekong River, away from Vietnam and into the refugee camps of Phnom Penh. Cambodia was in the last stages of a civil war, a brutal war of attrition.

"Undying," my father told us once, in admiration of the resistance, the Khmer Rouge.

"The undying," my mother answered, "are always the most wretched."

In January 1975, James's letters stopped. Three months later, the Khmer Rouge won the war and the borders closed around my country.

Turn my head, go back, and I'm hiding with my brother in the hall closet, crouched on top of my mother's shoes. "You'll see," my father is saying. We can hear his voice, tipsy and melodious, through the wooden door. "The Khmer Rouge will turn out to be heroes after all."

My uncles, great-uncles, and distant uncles shout to be heard. "Lon Nol," I hear. "Traitor!" "Crawling into bed!" "Contemptible!" "Chinese rockets!" My father's parties are always boisterous, more and more as the war goes badly. The North Vietnamese Army against the American military, the Khmer Rouge versus the Khmer Republic, Communism against Imperialism, everyone takes a side, and some take every side. My father says that this war is about the future, about a free Cambodia, that we have to liberate the country from our own worst selves. He says our leaders have lost their moral centre, they are obsessed with cognac and soda, and villagers' mumbo jumbo. The uncles cackle, and someone scratches at the door. I think it must be my cousin, Happy Nimol, who clings to us like wet grass.

The door bursts open and for a moment the room is stunningly bright. My father leans down, scoops my brother up. I see the pale soles of Sopham's feet kicking in the air. My father looks down at where I'm curled tight as ball. "Aha!" he says. "My little chickens, hiding from the farmer!" He carries us, laughing, screaming in terror, out into the gathering.

Years later, when I remembered the story of Vesna

Vulovic, I tried to find her in the archived newspapers of the Vancouver Public Library. As I turned the micro-film, an image, eerily familiar, stopped my hand: an exhausted face subsiding into white pillows. I paid for a printout of the image. Vesna's plane had been shot down by two surface-to-air missiles, fired by the Czechoslovak military because the Yugoslavian plane had crossed, innocently, into restricted airspace. "I'm not lucky," she said. "Everybody thinks I'm lucky, but they are mistaken. If I were lucky I would never have had this accident." She sounded ungrateful but she was not. I understood. I remembered arriving in Canada, my stomach clenched, ashamed that I had lived yet terrified of disappearing. Chance had favoured us, but chance had denied so many others.

At home, I taped Vesna's picture to my bedroom wall. For long stretches of time I would lie on the carpet, staring up at her. Sometimes I would see the shadows of Lena's feet, faint beneath the door. Like messages, I told myself. Missives. *Janie, sweetheart. Can I come in?* I was twelve when I arrived in Vancouver, when Lena became my foster mother. We'd sit and watch TV together, *The Nature of Things*, game shows, movies of the week, anything that might improve my English. But television, with its dizzying pictures and chaotic chatter, with its sudden images of love and violence, disturbed me. I turned instead to the shelves and shelves of books. Even though my reading was slow, painstaking, I worked my way through her collection. She was devoted to biographies – she admired mathematicians Kurt Gödel and Emma Noether and neuroscientists Santiago Ramón y Cajal and Alexander Luria.

To the surprise of my new mother, I stole these books as frequently as I stole canned food from the cupboards, and I hoarded all the words for myself. In my mind, it was as if these people walked through Lena's rooms, as if they were family and they were still alive.

Every weekend, Lena would descend into her office. "Down to the basement," she would say. "Down to my ballroom." Lena, an academic, wrote about the history of science. Her world was populated with mathematicians, physicists, chemists, and biologists, with the institutes and the drawing rooms of another era. Todd, my foster father, lived in Nepal and worked for Unicef, and he came home once each year, at Christmas. Some days, my new mother would spend hours sifting through piles of paper, trying to lay hands on a single reference. "Hopeless!" she would say, turning away from me, trying to mask her sadness. "Like trying to find a peanut floating through outer space."

From the time I was sixteen years old, I worked in the ballroom, helping Lena organize her documents. Not just papers, she would have said, but thoughts. Her office was a city all its own: towers of research notes, clippings, books, interview transcripts, recordings. I wanted to be of use to her, to repay her somehow. I liked the idea that I could stand in her place and find my way along the avenues she had built, the knowledge she had accumulated.

One night, wanting to surprise me, Lena dusted off the projector and sat me down in the living room. The sofa was covered with brown velour, a fabric unfamiliar to me, and I always felt as if I were sitting on an animal. The film spun into life. I gazed up, mesmerized by the world projected onto the white wall. I saw a much younger Lena walking on the beaches of Kep, on the southern coast of Cambodia. The camera closed in on Lena's bathing cap and her lemon-coloured dress. She and Todd had vacationed there in the 1960s, when Cambodia was at peace, a few years before the fighting had begun. She had never forgotten it, she told me, the heat, the saffron temples, the sea. She and Todd had been newlyweds.

Night after night, I crept downstairs, thieved the reels, and fed the film into the machine. I sat on the couch staring up, hearing only the ticking of the projector as the reels spun and the tape ran, and this clicking became the wordless sadness of a lost time. I saw the skyline and the light-flecked water, Lena's legs smooth against the ocean as she dove and dove again. In another reel, the city of Phnom Penh flickered grainily into the room. Todd, holding the camera, turned slowly, taking us in a 360-degree tour of the intersection in front of the

Central Market. Cars glided, cyclos wobbled through the field of vision, and families, clothed in oranges and pinks and browns, turned to stare into the lens. The images came one after the other, now in a place I recognized, and now not. There was no order, no chronology, yet it was so real I could smell it, I could feel the city's grit on my skin.

One night, I sat on the edge of Lena's bed and told her that I wanted a new name, a new existence, and she had stared at me, her eyes wet with tears. I admired those tears, she was not ashamed of them, or frightened by them. Jane. *Janie.* In the language of the aid world, I was an unaccompanied minor, a separated child, but Lena told me that I was no such thing at all. "Sometimes," she said, across the gap of space I kept between us on the bed, "we are granted a second chance, a third one. You don't have to be ashamed of having lived many lives."

I thought of my friend Bopha, about my brother, Sopham, and my parents, I wanted to tell Lena that we were too many, that I needed to guard the world that held us all together. I was afraid that I would drop it, shatter it, let it break apart.

The Khmer Rouge had taken Phnom Penh and then, quietly, they had gone around and severed the lines that connected us to the outside world. They named their own leadership, their own government, Angkar. The word means "the centre" or "the organization." In the beginning, our family had stayed together. But afterwards, when it was no longer possible, I tried to imagine a way back. Time had to be held, twisted, cut wide open.

Angkar had been obsessed with recording biographies. Every person, no matter their status with the Khmer Rouge, had to dictate their life story or write it down. We had to sign our names to these biographies, and we did this over and over, naming family and friends, illuminating the past. My little brother and I were only eight and ten years old but, even then, we understood that the story of one's own life could not be trusted, that it could destroy you and all the people you loved.

There is no air in the apartment, but I don't want to open the windows as I fear that the ice will come inside. I get up, throw a coat over my wrinkled clothes and a hat on my head. Out, out, out. Down the treacherous stairs, sliding along the invisible sidewalk. My brother is here. Sopham and I take the quiet streets, we file past the silent houses. I am drawn to the windows, to rooms lit by the inconstant blue of their televisions. A car swerves around me, the driver punctures the silence with his impatient horn, but I am moving with the slowness of the old. When I get too warm, I pull my hat off and hang it on the spoke of a fence. My brother walks ahead of me. He is small and thin and he finds the cold difficult. Where are his shoes? I look everywhere for them until my hands are numb with cold. Tomorrow I will not remember where my hat is, tomorrow

I will feel confusion, but for now I duck into St. Kevin's Church. On the bitterest winter nights, they leave the front doors unlocked. My brother trails behind me. I sink both hands into the holy water and bring my fingers to my eyes. We sit in the very last row and gaze at a man, kneeling in prayer, who seems to be thinking of the heavens, of the high windows that no one can reach, he is somewhere far, far above us. The smell of incense calms me. Long ago, I read that the cathedral in Phnom Penh had, in 1975, been dynamited. Even the very foundations were dug out, as if to prevent these foreign ruins from ever competing with our own. The vast temples of Angkor Wat, the old kingdoms of Funan and Chenla, were the markers of a history that went back two thousand years. All else, the Khmer Rouge insisted, was mere transience.

An elderly woman turns toward me. She comes closer along the pew and says, "I'm glad that you've come." Her white hair frames her head like a halo. She says, "You know that wonderful passage? It's always been my favourite. 'In my Father's house there are many rooms.'"

I feel myself trembling.

"You've been drinking," she says, compassionate. "Many of your people have this illness. But you've come home now. It will be all right."

I tell her that she is wrong, that even though we are surrounded by the sea, there is nothing to drink. Yet the salt water is seeping into our skin, swelling our bodies, making us unfit for land. "You know," I say. "Don't you?"

The woman hesitates, then she looks down at the boy in my lap who is nothing but a knotted, filthy scarf. Red-chequered, tattered. I unfold it and try to smooth the scarf against my legs. "I tried to save him," I tell her. "I tried to keep him from drowning." She looks up toward the high altar, the glowing lights, Jesus illuminated on his cross, then she gazes at me with understanding in her eyes. Sometimes it's pity, undeserved as it is, that hurts me most.

When the unthinkable happened, I had gone to Hiroji's apartment. Years ago, when he was travelling more frequently, he had given me a copy of his keys so that I could take care of Taka the Old. For nearly a month now I have slept on his couch, leaving the curtains open as if I believe he will re-enter through the unlatched windows. I know that he is in Cambodia, the place where his brother, James, was last seen. There is no other place he would go. I imagine him unpacking his suitcase, telling me what he has learned, all the things he has seen: the Tonle Sap reversing its waters, the sprawling jungle, bats high in the shadows of the caves. He will tell me how to accept this life. I dream of returning home, not only to the place of my birth but to my son. My mother who died without me, who died so long ago, will finally close her eyes. She will turn her gaze from this world, she will slide like a boat up against land, into her future.

—

In the morning, I walk to Kiri's school. From Monday to Friday, I see my son once each day, we meet in the playground before school begins. This is the routine Navin and I have worked out. It is an interim measure, we have both said. A way forward.

When I arrive, Navin is already there, leaning against the fence. I go to stand beside him. He touches my cheek. For a brief moment, his lips are warm against mine. "You didn't sleep last night," he says.

I tell him that I did, a little, enough. My hands are icy and Navin takes hold of them. He says that I look exhausted, that I should take some time off. "It's okay," I tell him. Work gives me a feeling of order, of cheer. He kisses my frozen fingers, and the kindness that I have always loved in him, that he gives so freely, washes over me. But Navin, too, is worn out.

I say again, "It will be okay."

In the playground, there are so many snowsuits in so many primary colours that my vision is temporarily dazzled. I stand at the fence and search the kaleidoscope for Kiri. There he is. I see him now, I see him. My son races across the grounds, a cub in a pack of awkward pups, pursuing a soccer ball. When his team scores, he howls with joy. The pink sky burns around us. Kiri chases the soccer ball, he tussles, fights, drops his hat, picks it up, and waves it like a flag.

"Did you get my message," Navin asks. "About Vancouver?"

I nod. "When will you go?"

"Next week, if I can pull everything together." He says he is just finishing up a project, a new building design, but his colleagues can oversee it. He thinks the distance will be good for Kiri. He says that Kiri keeps asking when I'll be coming home. "I'll talk to him," I say. We are surrounded by parents and children, by the rippling joy of the playground. Navin begins to say something but just then Kiri glimpses us. He runs forward. A girl stops him. "Kiri! Kiri!" she calls.

"I'm a caterpillar," he says.

She frowns, "No! You're not."

"I'm a worm," he says charmingly, and the girl waves both arms in kind of Hawaiian dance.

Kiri comes to me. I kneel down and he tells me, in a rush of words, that he's going to visit his Auntie Dina later, they're planning to build a rocket park, that she'll make him murtabak and roti canai, that her dog, Bruno, is kind of old and shuffles very slowly. Kiri has taken to speaking quickly now, as if he is afraid he will run out of time. As if he will be too late.

"Will you build a moon?" I ask him, kneeling in the snow. I busy myself readjusting his hat, which has fallen between his neck and the collar of his coat.

"Oh!" he says, surprised. "Good idea."

"What about moon boots?" Navin says. "Moon cakes?"

Kiri frowns.

"Moonlight," I say.

My son frees his hands and begins buttoning my coat up, all the way to the top. "Don't get cold, Momma," he says. I promise that I won't. His mittens, attached to his coat, swing back and forth like a pair of extra hands.

I kiss them both goodbye. They walk through the schoolyard, up the front steps of the building. Navin turns back, watching me, love and pity in his eyes. They go on, Kiri's hat bobbing up and down. In this way, my son is embraced by the glow of the school. Snow hurries forward to lay its thin white sheet over the teeter-totters, the swings, and the monkey bars. Through the big windows, I can see a movement of colours, children swirling around one another. Even at the edge of the schoolyard, I can hear their voices.

I catch the 535, heading downtown. The man next to me is nodding off to sleep, his body propped up by his fellow passengers. When the bus jumps, startling him awake, he looks up, surprised to see us. Rivulets of melted slush glide back and forth along the floor. In our heavy boots, we step daintily through the muck.

We arrive at my stop and I exit through the back doors. Above me, in the clearing sky, pigeons roost on the high wires, clouds descend, and I turn and walk east along the frozen skirts of Mount Royal. The mountain, dipped in snow, has an eerie beauty, tree after tree rising up the hill, slender as matchsticks. The temperature is dropping fast and people, blank-faced beneath their hats and scarves, shoulder roughly by. This place wears its misery so profoundly. Mean-eyed women, sheathed in stiletto boots, kick the ice aside while small men in massive coats lumber down the sidewalk. The elderly fall into snowbanks. All human patience curdles in the winter. On University Street, I turn left, continuing until I reach the heavy doors of the Brain Research Centre.

Sherrington, Broca, Penfield, Ramón y Cajal: in the atrium of the building, the names of our scientific fore-bears are etched in gold lettering along the wall. The wide hallways buzz with fluorescent light. Rather than going downstairs to my lab, I climb the stairs to the airy fourth floor where the clinicians hold court. The morning neurology and neurological surgery rounds are already underway and this hallway is temporarily deserted. I come to Hiroji's office. In January, the BRC disabled his code but not the code of our laboratory group. When I punch in the numbers, a green light blinks fleetingly before some mechanism clicks. I turn the knob and enter.

Here is Hiroji's window with a view of the mountain. Here is his desk.

I step inside, shutting the door behind me. File cabinets range against the right-hand wall, all the way to the ceiling. Morrin, the head of our research unit, has been pushing me to move our shared files from Hiroji's office, but I hadn't yet gotten around to it. I thought that, by the time I organized everything, Hiroji would be back and then the files, too, would have to return. There seemed no point in even beginning. The cabinets whine when I open them. Half of the contents are already gone, all the patient files have been moved elsewhere, but the entire history of our collaborative work remains, perfectly ordered.

I call Morrin's extension and tell him that, if he's looking for me, I'm in Hiroji's office, doing the dreaded deed. He says he'll bring up some boxes. When Morrin arrives, he, too, lingers for a moment. The three of us have spent many hours in here, discussing, arguing, idling. The office unnerves him. He goes to the window, glances out, and then returns to the relative safety of the door.

"Janie," he says. "Sorry to make you do this."

"You were right. It's time."

He nods. Weeks earlier, he had tried to draw me out on this subject, but I had rebuffed him. Now, he takes a pen from Hiroji's desk and taps it soundlessly against his fingers. He says that I should call downstairs if I need anything.

"A second brain?" I say.

He laughs. "Hmm. No, but there's a new dissecting scope. Come and see it when you're done." Still holding the pen, he leaves.

When all the files have been removed, I shut the cabinet and sit down in Hiroji's chair. The morning light, tipped in gold, has laid its gaze across the desk, illuminating a stapler, a box of paperclips, and a thumb-sized bronze Buddha in a seated posture, both hands extended in the gesture of protection. Hiroji has an object coveted by all the other neurologists: a phreno-logical map of the brain, drawn onto a porcelain head. During the Victorian era, the brain was believed to have forty-eight mental faculties, and each of these had a specific location that could be felt via bumps on the skull. *Destructiveness*, for instance, curves like a horse-shoe behind the ear. *Immortality* floats at the crown of the head, far above *vagrancy* and *animality*, low qualities that swell the neck. *Blandness* is neighbour to *agreeableness*. My own head has a bump above my left temple. Hiroji had studied the map.

"Mirthfulness," he had said, grinning, looking up.

We had both laughed. He used to rest his glasses on the head's porcelain nose, so much more upright, he said, more Roman, than his own.

I open the drawers. This trespass shames me, and yet I continue, running my fingers through the con-tents of his desk. In the middle drawer, I see a box of slides, various batteries, an adapter, and a half-finished roll of wine gums. Underneath all this is a small yellow notebook. Hesitantly, I reach for it, thinking that it might be a calendar or even a journal. When I open it, my friend's handwriting is so familiar, so known, that a surge of emotion hits me. Names, addresses, and num-bers fill every page. Under my own name, there are at least a dozen crossed-out entries, a decade-long list of all the cell phones I have lost and the apartments I have vacated. I see where Navin's name has been added to mine, or Naveen as Hiroji writes it, and then Janie/Nav/Kiri, so that we become variations of one another. Our names are accompanied by two exuberant exclamation points, which makes me suspect that Hiroji is beside me, pulling my leg. I continue through the alphabet. At the very end, on the inside back cover, is one last entry. *Ly Nuong.* Underlined once. Two numbers have been written beneath it, one appears to be North American and has been crossed out, but the second remains. It begins with +855, the country code for Cambodia.

I close the address book and put it back in the drawer. I carry the boxes downstairs, one by one. On the last trip, sweating, I return to the desk. I take out the address book and place it, carefully, into the box.

Evening arrives quickly. In the foyer where the BRC branches off to the hospital and the university, I sit, unable to face the freezing cold. This foyer is an intersection, a place where patients, neurologists, researchers, families, and students meet and part. I have been a researcher at the BRC for twelve years. Many floors below, in my electrophysiology lab, I have listened, hour after hour, to the firing of single neurons. In my work, I harvest cells, gather data, measure electricity while, in the upper floors, lives open and change: a patient with a brain tumour begins to lose her vision, a girl ceases to recognize faces, including her own, a man stares, disgruntled, at his left leg, refusing to believe that it belongs to his body. So many selves are born and re-born here, lost and imagined anew.

Now, a woman in a hospital gown has been brought to a halt, overwhelmed by the patterned lines on the floor. A nurse comes and prods her forward. My friend Bonnet, rushing by, catches sight of me. He asks me what I've been dissecting today and I tell him sea slugs. Bonnet, who works in brain imaging, and whom I often tease for walking fast to nowhere, is already halfway down the corridor. "How's your boy?" he says, walking backwards now. "Seems like ages since Kiri visited." I deflect. "You never weep for the sea slugs." He laughs, pirouettes in his lab coat, saluting me, and vanishes around the corner. The woman in the hospital gown is still walking, considering each line as it comes to her. Parkinson's, well advanced. The nurse says, "Are you sure you don't want a wheelchair, Nila?" The woman looks at me, aggrieved. "It's like being in a pram, isn't it? Why race to stand still? They won't bring the lunch trays for another hour yet."

As they move across the foyer, I retrieve the yellow book from my coat pocket. All afternoon, the name Nuong has been clamouring in my thoughts. I calculate the time difference once more. In Cambodia, tomorrow morning has arrived. I take out my phone and dial the international number. On the sixth ring, a woman answers.

I ask to speak to Ly Nuong.

When she doesn't respond, I ask a second time, switching to Khmer, though the words no longer come easily to me. She laughs, relieved, and says, No, Nuong isn't here, he's already left for work. She has a Phnom Penh accent, the same as my parents.

"Who is this?" she asks.

My English name feels awkward so instead I say, "I'm calling from Canada."

"Canada, yes. I will tell him."

I thank the woman and hang up. The phone feels heavy in my hand. I pick it up again and dial Meng's number. Though it rings for a long time, nobody answers.

The first time it happened, it was January. I had been anxious and overworked, and then, that day, I couldn't find my wallet, and then my keys. In the confusion, I forgot to pick Kiri up from daycare. By the time the aggravated staff reached me, my son had been waiting in the deserted rooms for more than two hours.

I ran all the way. At the daycare, I thanked the staff and apologized as best as I was able, then I took Kiri's hand and we made our way through the snow, stumbling together on the patches of ice. The sky was charcoal and the cold ambushed us. My son had lost his scarf. He asked me where I had been and when I didn't answer, he started to cry, he pulled on my hand but my body was light and my hand felt far away.

At home, I made dinner and he wandered around beside my legs, tugging at my clothes. "What's wrong, Momma?" he asked me over and over. In my head was a thick sadness, but I tried to concentrate on the rice and the carrots and then the faded green beans. I knew that if I spoke, my words would be slurred and broken so instead I tried to conserve my energy. My child began to weep. He picked up his cat and buried his face in her fur. There was a memory at the edges of my conscious-ness, but with a great force of will I managed to avert my eyes from it. I put rice and carrots and green beans into a small plastic bowl and I set the bowl carefully on the table. I stood in front of the stove for one long minute after another, trying to make certain that all the burners were off. Kiri asked for a spoon. I switched the dials on and off to make sure. I must do things in order. I walked through the darkness to the bedroom. Kiri's voice was far away, like the scuffling of mice between the walls. "What happened, Momma? Why are you crying?" I went to the bedroom and shut the door as softly as I could.

Jambavan was lying on my pillow. Kiri's cat watched me lazily. I liked her company. I remembered the day we brought her home, this tiny kitten who loved to nestle inside Kiri's sock drawer. Around the apart-ment, my son would crawl like a maniac, sputtering,

"Jambajambajamba." Navin said, "Sounds like a Latin dance." The name had been my idea, Jambavan, the king of bears, a hero of the Ramayana, the epic that, in Cambodia, we called the Reamker.

My son scratched at the door. "Can I make you dinner?"

"I love you, Kiri," I said. I could hear him sobbing for what felt like hours, and the sobbing was like a coat of skin that I wore, that I couldn't remove.

Navin came home to this wreckage and still he forgave me.

I wanted to tie my son's wrist to mine with a piece of string and in this way save us both. It's in the night, I know, that the ones we love disappear. Once, when I was ten years old, Kosal, the head of our cooperative, had given me the clothes of another girl. He told me to wear them out into the fields. Later on, when I undressed in the half-light, I saw that blood had seeped through the fabric and marked my skin, it covered my chest and my thighs. I remember the sound of water, my mother scrubbing the clothes over and over. I remember she scrubbed so hard the black dye came off in streaks. We wrote the girl's name on a piece of bark and buried it in the earth. My mother prayed for life. I looked at the sky, at the trees, at the disturbed mound of earth and saw no possible gods.

While Navin slept beside me, I fought to contain my thoughts. In my dreams, I saw everyone and everything, but never my mother, never Sopham. The Khmer Rouge had taught us how to survive, walking alone, carrying nothing in our hands. Belongings were slid away, then family and loved ones, and then finally our loyalties and ourselves. Worthless or precious, indifferent or loved, all of our treasures had been treated the same.

Outside, I am surrounded by tiny sequins of snow. I walk downhill on University Avenue, toward Café Esperanza, where inside, the heat welcomes me. The owner is washing the laminated menus, vigilantly, as if polishing fine silverware. He grimaces out the window at a man in yellow overalls, harnessed to a complicated system of belts and clasps, floating above the traffic. The man is part acrobat, part city worker, repairing the wires. The orange light of his truck spins over us like quiet laughter.

Hiroji

❖

In fits and starts, Hiroji tells me what has happened. It is March, not quite a year ago, nighttime, and we are sitting in his apartment.

On his way home from the BRC, Hiroji says, passing by Café Esperanza, he glimpsed an older Japanese man, moving slowly, dressed in a raincoat, with neither hat nor gloves. For a brief moment, the man looked at him. A shock of recognition stopped Hiroji where he stood. How could such a thing be possible? But there was no mistaking it.

The Japanese man was in his mid- to late sixties. His once-dark hair was now completely grey and there was a line, a scar, running from the corner of his right eye across his cheek. By the look of it, an old injury. He had the same high forehead, Hiroji said, and slight, dark eyes, but his body had gone brittle and crooked. His jacket was far too thin and the scarf he wore was ineffectual, open at the neck and hanging loose like an unknotted tie. Hiroji stared at the stranger and he knew, instantly, that it was his brother. That it could not be his brother. And yet, that it was.

"Wait," the man said. "I know you."

"Ichiro," Hiroji said. Cold air caught in his lungs. "James."

"You remember! It's astonishing. Come have supper with me."

"Tonight? But I have plans." Hiroji hardly knew what he was saying. The older man seemed insubstantial, a reflection of a reflection.

"Just a coffee, then. Please. We must, after all these years."

In the distance was an electric sign flashing sharp red digits. He could just make it out: nearly five in the afternoon, minus 22 centigrade. Hiroji felt his legs beginning to give way. "All right. Just a coffee."

They passed through the doors of Café Esperanza. On the counter was a cake stand with a glass cover, inside of which curled a half-dozen croissants. Hiroji bought them all and, at first, the older man, ravenous, ate without speaking. He dipped the croissants one by one into his bowl of café au lait until the serving plate held only crumbs. Then he licked the tip of his index finger, pressed it to each of the remaining flakes, and ate those too.

"You eat croissants just as the Parisians do," Hiroji said.

The man looked up, crumbs on the corners of his mouth, pleased, almost childlike, at the thought. "Maybe I was one. Maybe that's who I was, in my other life."

In the warm interior light, the man looked younger. He smiled in a way that seemed giddy and unfamiliar.

"Forgive me," Hiroji said, embarrassed. "I'm very sorry, but I can't seem to remember how we met."

"I thought you knew me! You said my name."

"You seemed familiar to me."

Upset, the man began to ramble. He was soft-spoken, and Hiroji had to lean forward to catch all the words. The man described waking, suddenly, on the wet ground, his entire body convulsed with pain. Things were broken, blood was sticky on his fingers, but he couldn't remember why, he didn't know how this had happened. For hours, maybe days, he had walked in a dream, not comprehending how things moved in the world. Cars hurried down on him. There were too many voices speaking too many languages and he didn't know which one belonged to him. His stomach hurt and his legs felt empty, but he didn't know that this hollowness was hunger. He had no memories, no thoughts, no ideas, nothing. Everything had been taken away, that much he understood, but by whom and when did it happen? He walked to the middle of the Pattullo Bridge and stood there for a long time and the river kept flowing, he saw timber bobbing on the surface, log booms and log traffic, a gull standing on a bit of rope, and he had the sensation that both sides of the river were tightening like a vise. Someone had tricked him, someone had come in the night and robbed him of his possessions.

"I got up on the railing," he told Hiroji. "I looked at the world and I thought, What now? What happens now? I wasn't angry. I just wanted to stand there and ask my question. I wanted someone to acknowledge me."

He stared up at the lights of the café, wild-eyed.

The man was starving. Hiroji caught the waitress's attention and asked if there was any more food to be had. The girl was young and she gazed at them with curious eyes. She returned with a few slices of bread, an enormous hunk of cheese, and a little dish of jam. "The owner's fridge," she said. "But he won't be back until after the weekend."

The man ate intently.

"Someone found you and brought you to the hospital," Hiroji said. He had a glimmer, now, of a patient he had long forgotten.

The man swallowed the bread that was in his mouth. He reached for a water glass that wasn't there, then let his hand rest limply on the table. "The others called me John. Johnny Doe. That was unkind, wasn't it? A name that shouts that no one's home. Useless. You called me James."

"But it was long ago, wasn't it?"

The man smiled. "You're asking me? That seems a problem, Doctor. Did you fall and hit your head too? It must be thirty years at least."

"I remember that we discharged you."

"I've done all the tests: PET, SPECT, fMRI, EEG. Even

a polygraph, in case I was just a liar." He picked up a piece of bread, wiped it in the remaining jam, and then added the last rectangle of cheese. "I met a woman from St. John. I met her at the theatre. She invited me to her house for a visit. I could make it there tomorrow but I have no money for the bus."

"Where do you live?"

The older man shook his head. He stared at the waitress, who had her back to them, wiping down the machines.

"I'll pay you back," he said. "Believe me. I'm good for it. If I stay in St. John and find work . . . that's tough at my age but I have skills, good skills. I wasn't from Vancouver, was I? Nobody knew me, but you and I, we were friends. I sounded American, Californian, that's what you said. Maybe San Francisco, you said. Some things stick. You were friendly to me, as if I were a whole person and not a zero. A waste."

Hiroji didn't know what to say. His memories of treating this man were tenuous, almost nothing.

"Wait here a moment," he said at last as the man continued to gaze at him. "Don't go anywhere, please."

The man smiled down at his lap. "Oh, I'm in no hurry."

Hiroji went across the road to a bank machine and he withdrew six hundred dollars. The cash went into a deposit envelope, which he sealed, with difficulty, and then he ran, slipping, across the pavement, between the pedestrians and their shopping bags and groceries.

He fell on the ice, but through his coat he felt no pain. At the café, he gave the envelope to the man, who accepted it solemnly. Then Hiroji paid the waitress, tipping her generously. He hailed a taxi for James or Johnny or California, and he gave the driver money too. All he had was money.

"Don't worry," the man said, holding Hiroji's business card between his fingers. "I'll return the favour. Wait a few days."

"No," Hiroji said. "It's fine."

The wheels of the taxi spun on the snow, then the car pulled away.

"I started walking," Hiroji told me. All the way, he kept replaying the encounter in his head, the way this man, this patient, had counted his words out, like his brother used to do when he was drinking, as if he meant to spend the sentences wisely. He thought that his brother must be alive somewhere. He could be wandering, just wandering. He remembered, now, how the patient—Johnny, James—had been persuaded to come down from the railing of the Pattullo Bridge. He had been thirty-five years old at the time, older maybe. Someone had whacked him hard at the back of the head, so violently that his brain had crushed up against the front part of his skull. They had not been able to help him. Someone had joked, carelessly, that the two young men, Hiroji Matsui and Johnny Doe, the two Japs, looked like brothers. It had not been funny and nobody had laughed.

We were sitting at his kitchen table. Hiroji had opened a bottle of champagne and now he drank it like tap water. "I still remember the name of the doctor who made that joke," he said, his voice shaking. "He's dead now, but I still remember. I remember."

He put his glass on the coffee table, went to the sideboard, and returned with a file. Inside were letters he had received from James, sent from Cambodia. The airmail paper was decades old, the sheets dry and ready to crumble, the Red Cross insignia faded. "I went there, to the border," Hiroji said. His voice was insistent, upset. "I went to Aranyaprathet, to the refugee camps, to Sa Kaeo, I lived in Aran, I took care of a boy, Nuong. I loved Nuong like my own son but even he was lost. I came back without him. My mother asked me, 'Where is your brother? Where is Ichiro?' I told her, 'We have to wait.' 'Wait for what?' she asked. There was nothing I could say."

I remembered Phnom Penh the day I walked out of it, the day the war ended. I saw the assault rifle against my father's stomach, the way the barrel pushed him viciously against the wall.

"When my mother died," he said, "I stopped looking. I wanted to be free of him."

I told Hiroji, "You did everything possible."

His hair, normally so immaculately in place, had fallen forward over his eyes. "I'm old now. I foolishly think that he . . . I dream about him. Do you find that strange?"

"No."

Hiroji swayed slowly to his feet. He looked around the room as if he didn't know where to go, to the couch or to the window, or even farther. Behind him, the blinking Christmas lights, up since December, dabbed the walls with colour, rhythmic and persistent.

I said, as gently as I could, "It wasn't possible to save your brother. It wasn't possible to save many people."

For a moment my eyes watered. His expression changed, guilt-stricken now. Ashamed. I wanted so much to help him, to make him understand that there was nothing we could do. We had to let go. "I only mean that it's difficult to find one person. It's difficult. For you, for me, for anyone."

"Forgive me, Janie. It's my foolishness, nothing more."

"No. Don't say that."

We fell into silence. He went to the table, took the champagne bottle, and refilled my glass. It frothed over the lip and ran between my fingers.

"Hiroji," I said. "Listen. If you could have seen Phnom Penh that day. Or afterwards. If you knew what it was like." I remembered my brother, his thin shoulders. To end up in one of the Khmer Rouge prisons meant that a person would die alone, in torment that was unimaginable. You had to hope that a brother, a father, died before reaching that point. You had to hope for the best.

"I know, Janie," he said. He stood up unsteadily, lifting his plate.

"Wait," I said.

"I'm not myself. I wasn't thinking."

I got up to help him but he said no, he asked me to sit for a moment. He went into the kitchen. I could hear Hiroji scraping the plates off, setting them in the sink. The file remained on the table. I slid it toward me. In the kitchen, the water ran thinly. Alone in the dining room, I began to sift cautiously through the pages. They were translations of Khmer documents, correspondence with various government officials, maps. Pages and pages of requests for information.

"Right," Hiroji said when he came back into the room. "Don't ever let me host a party again." He smiled at me, reached out, rested his fingertips against my shoulder for a moment. He saw the pages spread across the table and, embarrassed, began to gather them up.

I stilled his hands. "Let me."

I put everything, the maps, the letters, back into the file. It was full. Hiroji had been seeking information for years, but despite his efforts he had never found any trace of his brother. He began speaking about the Documentation Centre of Cambodia, DC-Cam he called it, an institution that was collecting documents related to the Khmer Rouge.

"Do you mind if I take these?" I said. "I could call them. It might be easier for someone who speaks the language, who knows the country." I knew that searching was futile, that James was gone. He was one of the many, one of the two million dead. Still, I thought that if I did my best, if I came back empty-handed, it might bring Hiroji some release.

He looked at me, surprised. Grateful.

Together, we went to the door and I proceeded to wrap the layers around me, coat, scarf, hat, gloves. Bundled up this way, I leaned forward to kiss him.

"Thank you for the gift, Janie," he said. "It is a wonderful gift."

On the sidewalk, I turned back once. He was still watching me, I could see the narrow doorway and the frail silhouette that he cast.

That week, I contacted DC-Cam and was put in touch with a researcher named Tavy. She had been working for the centre since it opened nearly a decade ago, cataloguing prison records, photographs, biographical information, and witness statements, documents that might be used in the upcoming War Crimes Tribunal. But, primarily, she told me, her job was to help Cambodians trace their missing family members. On the telephone, I struggled with words that should have come easily, but Tavy was patient. She said she would try to find James Matsui in the meticulous records of the Khmer Rouge. As the months went by, we spoke intermittently. There was never any new information. "Is there something more?" she asked me once. "I feel that there's something more you wish to ask me." I couldn't answer at first, and then, finally, I told her, "No, nothing." She said, "I understand." By then, I knew, clearly, that the search for James would lead nowhere. I stopped by Hiroji's apartment and tried to return the file. It was August. He asked me to hold on to it for a little while longer.

In the fall, he went to Leipzig, a guest of the Max Planck Institute. Every week, he telephoned me, he gave me detailed descriptions of the city, once home to Bach, Hertz, and Heisenberg. He said he strolled in the Botanical Garden every evening. James's letters had opened something in me, and I began sliding into a numb melancholy. The world seemed bled of colour, yet I had vivid, exhausting dreams. I felt as if I had realized some truth, returned to someone I longed for, just at the moment of waking. On Hiroji's return, in late October, we took a walk together through Mount Royal where, at the top of the mountain, we saw the evening lamps coming on. I remember how the oratory, St. Joseph, held the sun the longest, while everything below it slid into a coppery twilight. For the first time in many weeks, Hiroji brought up the subject of James. By then, I had set the file and its contents aside. I told Hiroji what I believed, that no matter how much we wished for it, no matter what we did, some ghosts could never be put to rest.

Hiroji nodded. "Maybe James would have said the same."

The mountain fell into dusk. We let the subject go. For the rest of the evening, we talked about our various projects. He directed me to studies I had not yet come across, he promised to put me in touch with researchers he had met in Germany.

Weeks passed.

I invited him to dinner at a restaurant in our neighbourhood. Before leaving home, I slipped the file into my bag, promising myself that I would return it to him.

Over the course of two hours we spoke in a careful way about work and the weather, about the headlines and the wars. It was a frosty November evening. I had never seen him look so energized, so strangely bright. But his hands were nervous.

"Are you sleeping well?" I asked.

"It's funny," he said. "Sleep feels like the last thing that I need."

Throughout the meal, I wanted to bring up James, the file, but I didn't know how. Eventually we bogged down in silence.

"Nuong called," he said, catching me by surprise. "He's living in Phnom Penh now."

He saw my confusion.

"The boy I took care of in Aranyaprathet, in the refugee camp. Do you remember? Nuong. He's around your age. He was adopted by a family in Massachusetts, back in 1981. Anyway, he's moved back to Phnom Penh. I was thinking that I could put you in touch with him. He can help us find James."

Hiroji kept speaking but the words didn't register. I took a sip of water, a bite of food, and then I put down my fork.

"Morrin says you've been in the clinic constantly this month. He says you're working all the time."

"I'm fine."

"You're not sleeping. You haven't even touched your food."

The restaurant was full now and the noise pressed in on us.

"Would you come with me?" he asked. "If I went to see Nuong. Could you come with me?"

November. It was the beginning of the dry season in Cambodia. Drenched fields, a slow, thirsting heat. I saw it all with a clarity that shook me. Hiroji's eyes seemed lighter, joyful. I looked away, ignoring his question. I couldn't hear my own thoughts. I leaned down, picked my bag up from off the floor, and withdrew the file.

He leaned forward.

"I'm sorry," I said. "I tried, but I couldn't get anywhere with it. There's no information to find. There's nothing." The words came out wrong. They came out thinly, dismissively.

He took the file, holding it in his hands for a moment as if he did not fully recognize it.

"I can't abandon him again."

"There isn't any other choice," I said. "We have to let them go."

His bag, a leather satchel, hung on the back of his chair. He opened it and put the file clumsily in. A waiter, hurrying by, bumped Hiroji's elbow and the bag fell. Some pages scattered on the floor. He leaned down, reaching toward them, the waiter kneeling to help him.

When he had gathered everything, Hiroji took out his wallet. He pressed a hundred-dollar bill into my hand. "Take this and buy a birthday present for Kiri."

Kiri's birthday was still a month away. I shook my head, upset.

"Take it," he insisted. "I had an antique microscope for him, but I couldn't get it repaired in time."

"He's only six. How could it matter if it's late?"

"It matters," he said. He signalled for the bill.

I asked him to come for coffee, to see me tomorrow or the day after. He said he was busy. "I'm behind," he told me. "I've let things get away from me." He signed the bill and turned it over so that it was face down. Some feeling between us had been extinguished but it would not last, I thought. I would repair it, I would make him understand. "Janie," he said when we parted. "Don't judge me too harshly." The words were pleading. "I have many regrets."

A week later, when I couldn't reach him on the phone, I went to his apartment. Inside, everything was neat and orderly. The cat had food and water to last for another week but, still, she ran to me crying. On the kitchen table, I found the file. He had left it behind, along with his driver's licence, his bank cards, and the hundred-dollar bill he had tried to give me for Kiri's birthday. I put all of these things into my bag, I packed up Taka the Old and took her home with me. From there, I called the police.

Mei

❖

The next morning, before dawn comes, I walk out onto the wide boulevard of Côte-des-Neiges where the queue for the downtown bus winds along the sidewalk, serpentine, a half-dozen men and women lost inside their winter coats, a light snow falling on us, as fine as sand. I ask someone what day it is, and he says, "Tuesday. One more Tuesday." He smiles and points out something on the horizon. The bus arrives and, gratefully, the people climb inside.

I begin walking, unsure where to go. I smell coffee from a nearby bakery, I see my little brother and myself, and the smell of bread permeates the air. We are caught outside when the air raid sirens begin. I try to pull him away. It is last night's memory, when mortar fire started and the rockets began to fall, the middle of the hot season, the beginning of the last Khmer Rouge offensive. There is a shelter nearby, a dry, shallow well in which we sometimes hide, but in my panic I can't find it. Instead, Sopham and I crouch against the wall of a building. He is carrying his drawing pencils in a blue cloth bag. The air turns to gas and the sidewalk heaves, splitting apart. I hold on to my brother, gripping him as if he is the world itself and an explosion will claim us together or not at all. His screaming becomes a wide emptiness, a pressure in the air blinding me, and in the darkness I hear a strange, familiar ticking – insects, the typewriter, a clock counting time, the melody of a piece of music – and then my brother repeating my name. He wipes my face with the sleeve of his shirt. The air explodes me from its grip and suddenly I see blood everywhere. *Run*, I hear him saying. *Sister, sister. Come with me.* Words begin to pour from him. He says there is another song he has learned but he cannot remember it, cannot remember. "My pencils," he says, "look at my pencils." But when I look all I see is the river, brown and churning, and a yellow boat idling, impossibly, on the surface. "Are you hungry?" he says. He asks me to find bitter *sdao* shoots for him to eat. I reach for the little purse in which I keep American coins but when I reach inside, the coins burn my fingertips. My brother takes the purse, turns it over, scatters the coins on the ground, and when I look down it seems as if they are writhing, they are melting on the road. We leave the money where it is and walk and walk, and my brother comes across a book of Buddhist prayers. We start laughing when we see it, the book seems like a trick of our father's who often recited verses when he was drunk, when he had gambled our money away, as if beautiful lines would save him in the eyes of our mother. Still, he would come armed with verses, unfurling them like peacock feathers, dazzling the eyes so we would be blind to the fear and anxiety below. My brother carries the book and we walk on, calling for our father and then, out of the smoke, he appears and runs to us. It is unbelievable, it seems a miracle that he could appear just because we say his name. He raises my brother high, sets him on his shoulders, then he picks me up and begins to run.

"The bombs are coming," I tell him. "They are coming, they are coming."

I feel my legs floating, as if I am flying through the streets.

I'm standing at the intersection of Côte-des-Neiges and Queen Mary, snow settling on us, and a woman tells her child, *We are safe as houses*. The saying falls straight through me. The light turns green, nothing approaches, I begin to walk, and the low buildings seem to bend over me. I see my father in the shape of another person, walking up ahead. I see the suit of clothes he used to wear, the haircut he had, his briefcase and his scuffed, worn-down shoes. I run up to the man who is not my father, grab his elbow, and spin him around to face me. A stranger swears and flings me away.

I am home again, inside the safety of our apartment, my father is standing behind me, dictating the words I have to transcribe. When I type, I feel the machine as an extension of my hands, my father's voice is rainfall, and I am a weed lifting up too fast, gangly and hungry and gaping in every direction. That typewriter, that gift, is my first real possession. Sometimes when I type, I pay attention to the words themselves, what they say and mean, but other times they are only strings of letters, arranged like beads, joined together by the metronome of the Olivetti. The words materializing on the page, this alphabet so different from the shivering, dancing Khmer script, seemed to me like crevices I could peer through, portholes into lives different, more gracious, than my own.

Someone says my Canadian name. *Janie*. Another woman turns and waves. I am standing in Montreal, on a white winter day, beneath unfamiliar buildings. I look everywhere for Janie. There are no trees, no forest anywhere, nothing to keep the light from falling through.

My father is a storyteller. He smiles and whispers at us to follow him, behind the curtain, into this starlit box. Hanuman, my favourite hero, wraps his giant hands around my little fingers. Tonight, he says, we will travel the world with Jambavan, the king of bears. My father can recite all the shiny strands of the Ramayana, he cajoles my brother and I with brave musketeers, with Tum and Teav and Molière. He gives us any story we ask for, especially tonight, because on this night, he says, the war is ending. Rocket fire burns the skies but tomorrow everything will change. Even as the shells fall down, our neighbours are dancing and welcoming the Khmer new year.

On the balcony, I sat down, leaning against my father's body. I was afraid and I didn't want to be apart from him. Fighting chipped away at the edges of the city, and Sopham pointed out the smoke advancing from the north, south, and west, like a necklace tightening. Tracer fire threw long lines into the darkness.

My father cradled his whiskey and called for the Communists to hurry up, to end the war once and for all. "Once the guns go quiet," my father said, "the Khmer Rouge will put everything right. Then you, my dancing, *kralan*-eating children, will go back to school. No more running wild. No more fighting in the streets." Our prime minister, otherwise known to us as Magic Sands, had fled the country. *Monsieur le sableur des feés*, our father called him, who defended our city with holy grains, who armed our soldiers with Buddhist scarves. Magic Sands had already been evacuated.

"Remember this night," he said. "Mark it in your memories because tomorrow everything changes." He smiled and shook his head and swirled the liquid in his glass. "Tomorrow, when your mother puts on her New Year's finery, she'll be the most beautiful woman in the city. The war is finished, little ones. We'll gather all the sadness into a pot, pour it down the drains, and hear it rush into the sea. The king will wake up in the Royal

Palace, and everything will be just as it was. As wonderful and as corrupt as it ever was." He lay down, staring up at the sky. Beads of sweat trickled down his face, into his hair.

"I should have gone to France," my father told us. "I should have carried your mother to Paris and we would have been poor together. You two, you and Sopham, you would have been born in the West, like champions!"

"Champions of what?" I asked.

"Champions of champions," my brother said.

"We would have flown Air France," my father said. "Just like that, on top of the world, sipping champagne. We would have set Europe on fire: your mother and your father, the beauty and the poet."

"And me, Pak?"

"You, Sopham? The singer, of course." My brother, frowning, did the twist for us.

"And me?"

What did he say? I try to remember.

Side by side, we stared up at the darkness, at the beckoning stars, doorways to other worlds and other galaxies. My father turned toward me, as if trying to read the future from my expression. He had curving, lifting, furrowing eyebrows. "You'll be like the great Hanuman, leaping across oceans. Between you and the heavens, my sweet, nothing will hold you back."

—

We heard someone running up the stairs. My mother was in the kitchen, making lunch, when the door behind her gave way. I saw a yellow knot in my brother's fist, round as the sun, and then, behind it, a black shape against the wall. The shining darkness of a rifle, an AK, the barrel finding its way across the room. It buried itself in my father's stomach.

"Wait," my father said softly. "Wait."

The boy stepped back. He swung the gun up and took aim at my father's chest. More Khmer Rouge came in, they were faceless to me, black pants, black shirts, muddy feet, too big to fit inside the room. First they were in the kitchen, then beside me, then at the window.

Outside, a woman started screaming. "He's not a soldier! It had nothing to do with him. Stop, please stop!" Gunfire then, drowning everything out.

"What is it?" my father said. I saw his mouth moving but his voice seemed to come from somewhere else. The soldiers pushed nearer. They were children, maybe teen-agers, with small, lean bodies. "What work do you do?" the boy asked him.

"I'm a translator."

"For the government?"

"No. Books, textbooks."

The boy's eyes drifted over my mother, over us.

"You have to evacuate the city," he said. "All of you. Don't take your things. You won't be gone long. Three or four days at the most. The Americans are going to bomb us."

"But why?" my father said, confused. "The war is over. They've already pulled out."

The boy nudged his rifle up, pushing it against my father's neck. "Take only the things you need," he said, "nothing more. Don't waste any time."

When they left, the door, broken off its hinges, swung wide. My father's hands travelled over his face, down his shirt. No bullet hole, no blood. He looked at his hands in disbelief. My mother told us to sit down at the table, to eat our food now, quickly, to come away from the windows, to come now, to hurry.

I followed my parents into the street. I thought the buildings, the hospitals, the banks and restaurants, the temples and market had all been tipped sideways, spilling everyone and everything into the road. There was no space to go back, to change direction, there was no room to breathe. I saw defeated soldiers wearing pristine uniforms, thin monks, lost children, rich men and poor men, I saw bodies curled on the sidewalk. Towers of rifles, strung with ammunition, lay jumbled on the street corners.

Our neighbour, Uncle Samnang, sat on the ground with a woman in his arms, weeping. "What happened to Uncle Samnang?" I asked.

My mother tilted my chin up, averting my eyes.

Money floated along the street, it flew up in bundles, dry and perfect, swirling above us. Sopham and I waved our hands to gather the bills. Everyone was talking but I didn't understand, I heard names that I didn't recognize, I looked up and saw the frangipani, pink as my mother's silk shoes. In the midday heat, their heads drooped low, their fragile necks were bent. "I'm thirsty," my brother said. We both carried small overnight bags. The straps rubbed against my shoulders. All I could smell was the sweetness of the flowers. My parents whispered to each other, back and forth, back and forth. We plodded on, stopping all the time because the crowd kept thickening, more and more people herded into the street. At the turnoff to Tuol Kok, my parents led us down an alleyway, into a courtyard. My grandfather's house slouched down, all the shutters closed. My mother went inside. White sheets, white flags, hung from all the balconies, motionless in the hot air.

A woman stood in the shade, her blouse dark with sweat. She told us that all the hospitals had been emptied, the injured and dying had been thrown into the street wearing their hospital gowns, holding their own IV bags. Government soldiers had been shot on the road, students and teachers were being trucked away.

"They told us not to pack very much," my father said sternly. "We'll come home in a day or two."

The woman's long hair had fallen loose and it clung to her neck. "They told me, 'Go back to your home village.' Well, mine is up past Battambang, that's three hundred kilometres away, and I haven't been there since I was a girl. Getting there will take more than a few days, won't it? And then what?"

My mother was standing in the doorway now. "He's gone," she said. "The doors are all broken. He's already gone."

We stood together, waiting in front of the house. A group of Khmer Rouge came and told us to get out of here, to move on.

The woman wandered off, scratching madly at her arms. "Watch your step," she said. "Don't fall into the holes."

Back on the main road, the crowd trudged slowly, as if through mud. A voice, amplified by loudspeakers, prodded us north, then west.

Beside me, a man with no legs crawled forward on his elbows. My mother was crying noiselessly. I stared at the ground and then up at the sky, where the elegant buildings seemed to wilt in the heat. I saw white shutters, cars turned on their sides, crates of chickens, howling dogs, and, in every direction, a shifting wall of people. On my left, two Khmer Rouge were guarding an intersection. I wanted to see them, I tried to get nearer.

A woman was arguing with them. She wanted to take another road but they were refusing to let her pass. She persisted. "My husband and children were sent down Route 2," she said. "If I hurry, I'll be able to join them."

She put her hands together, bowed her head, touched her fingertips to her forehead in a sign of respect. Casually, one of the boys lifted his rifle and shot her. She was thrown backwards, her skull cracking against the pavement. Blood poured from her heart as if it would never stop. Within seconds, the boys had unclasped her watch, taken her necklace and her ring, and then rolled the body to the edge of the road. The woman's hands still moved, her lips were speaking. One of the boys met my stare. "What are you looking at?" he said. He prodded the woman with his foot. "Does this belong to you?"

My father spoke my name, he pulled me away into the thicket of bodies.

My father disappeared. But still, even now, I imagine seeing him again. In my dreams, he tells me that time ran away from him. Time, only time. One day he blinked his eyes and thirty years had come and gone. Just last night, my father had knocked at my door, surprised and embarrassed, asking me where everyone had disappeared to, demanding to know why we hadn't waited and why, all these years, we had never answered his calling.

"You didn't have time to speak," I said.

"Didn't I?"

"On that day, it happened so quickly."

"I had a list of things to tell you," he said. There was snow in his hair, crystals on his eyelashes. "I had a list of things to tell little Sopham. Where is my boy? Where is Mother?" He stared at me, as if seeing me for the first time. "Why are you all alone here?"

Three days after we had begun walking, we reached a checkpoint. The men were separated and questioned one by one. Afterwards, my father was guided, alongside dozens of others, into a waiting truck, the soldiers pushing him into the vehicle as if he were a child. We lost sight of him but I heard him saying our names, my father's thin voice rising out of the press of bodies.

"Are you afraid of us?" one soldier asked, circling the truck. "Why in the world are you afraid, my brothers? When did we ever betray you?"

"Let me down," an old man said. "Please. I can't breathe. There's no air in here."

A boy aimed his AK at the truck and told the man to be still. He called him *mit*, my friend, comrade, he said that the men in the truck were the lucky ones. They were going into the forest to study, they were educated men who would one day serve the country and Angkar.

"But what is Angkar?" the old man asked.

The boy looked at him, incredulous. "Angkar fought this war and won your freedom. Don't you know?" He kept talking about Angkar, which meant the "organization," and Angkar Leu, the "Greater Organization." I understood the boy's words but I couldn't follow their meaning, it was as if another vocabulary, another history, had distorted the language I knew.

My mother went from one soldier to another, pleading with them to release my father. "Please," she said desperately. "Let him stay with us." Her hands were clasped together.

A soldier pushed her hands down. "Don't beg," he said. "Don't demean yourself. Everyone is equal now."

Sweat ran down my neck, down my back, it shone on the faces of the men as they bowed their heads against the sun. I heard my name spoken again and again, my father's voice calling as if he wanted me to join him, or flee, or hold on. The Khmer Rouge watched us with such derision, such contempt, I couldn't move, my limbs were frozen but things around me seemed to move faster, to grow tumultuous. Our religion was Buddhism and it taught us that life was suffering and that the cycle was eternal and would continue no matter our individual destinies. For the first time in my life, I saw the cycle, I saw its end, a lake, a nothingness on which we hovered.

The engine started and the truck pulled away. The soldiers watched until the men had disappeared, and then they lowered their guns.

My mother held us. She spoke into my brother's hair, "It's the dust, it's the dust, my darling. Who will help us? All I can see is dust."

The soldiers sent us south then east, then north again. Every night, we slept in the open, surrounded by hundreds of people until, bit by bit, the city people were gradually dispersed. There was a mountain, I remember, Phnom Chisor, that we skirted and climbed and descended, it was always there, growing larger or receding behind us. The farther we walked, the more silent the world became, stripped of traffic, blaring radios, air raid sirens, voices. Each morning, I woke believing my father had returned, but it was always my brother, prodding me awake, his eyes wide and alarmed. I saw purple skies, Martian seas against the saffron temples. I saw my mother trying to make a meal from the things we had scavenged. After weeks of walking, we were ordered to turn around, we were sent east across the river, into Prey Veng province.

My brother asked me if this wandering would last forever. Maybe the cities are truly gone, I said, and they have no place to send us. Gone how? he asked. Bombs, I said, but we had seen no airplanes, no fighters in the sky. He knew it, too, but didn't say so.

The rainy season began. Somewhere near to Wat Chroy, a man met us on the road. By then, we were a group of sixty or seventy people. The man, who said his name was Kosal, had eyes that seemed to droop at the edges, as if his face could be nothing but sad. He said he was the Angkar here and that this cooperative was our destination. We looked around: we were standing in a fallow field, at the edge of a tattered village.

"What do you mean?" someone asked. "Our homes are in Phnom Penh."

"Your homes are here," Kosal said, smiling kindly. "Angkar wants you to remain with us."

"But our belongings –"

Kosal nodded. "Tomorrow we'll think about the rest. *At oy té.* You have nothing to fear."

Staying near to one another, we made our camp for the night.

A teenaged boy was sent to guard us. He was tall, no more than fourteen years old, with an angular, mischievous face and a rifle slung across his back. He tapped the gun nervously, unable to keep his hands still.

The night sky came nearer, it was a cloth tightening around us, erasing the world. In my dreams, I saw bodies everywhere, infants and grown men, a wide-eyed girl, my brother, men built like steamships and others like sticks. I saw them all, as if we were on a road together, one body growing from the next, soaking into the ground. Above us, sugar palms stretched thinly up in the sky, into streaks of blue and golden light. I saw village houses, seated in a row. Here at our destination, I was the only one alive. I couldn't move or speak, fear was a shunt in my chest, I wanted to cry out but I couldn't even breathe.

I woke. I saw the tall boy with the gun, asleep against a tree, his mouth open, round like a baby's.

"That boy," my mother said, her voice low. "There's something familiar about that boy."

Our first day here began. We built three bare structures to shelter our group, and we covered each with a roof made of thatched palm leaves. They were dry and tough, my hands bled from weaving them together, everybody's hands bled because we were city people used to paper, pens, and smooth typewriters. There were teachers, students, a dentist, a banker, drivers, machinists, a hotel manager, there were families like ours where the father had been sent away, there were dozens of children. Villagers came and went, watching us. Cautiously, my brother approached them. He asked them to advise us on the proper knitting of the leaves, and a boy his age stopped to help us. Sopham, my small, earnest brother, worked hard, harder than all the rest.

At mid-day, the banker came and sat beside us. He had joined our group only a few days before, but we had never seen him sober. Along the way, he had traded all his extra clothes for rice wine. "Slow down, child," he said to my brother. "You must try not to draw attention to yourself."

Sopham looked up. After a moment he said, "I don't want to sleep in the open tonight. Smell the air, Uncle. It's going to rain."

"Which one of these men is your father?" the banker asked.

"They sent him to study."

"To study," the banker said. "Sent with his hands tied behind his back. Sent to the forest where there is no electricity, no school, no teachers, no books. Is that how an educated man studies? What theories will he

memorize there?" He smiled at us because he was unhappy. "My eldest boy is one of them," he said. "He
went to fight with these jungle Communists but I always
warned him, the Khmer Rouge are less than human, they
have no soul, no *pralung*. They'll cut your throat before
they introduce themselves —"

"How dare you," my mother said.

He looked up, startled.

"Get away from my children."

"But, madam," the banker said. "Have I said something untrue?"

Other voices hurried forward. *Lower your voices. Those
are rumours, only rumours. Can't you see he's drunk?* They
drew protectively around us, shutting him out.

"I've drunk nothing!" the banker said, shouting now.
"Go on then, keep playing. Make your little houses! You
have my pity." He stood up, smoothed his clothes, and
walked unsteadily away. My mother stared after him.

I saw the teenager with the gun watching us, an
amused smile on his lips.

That night, we huddled together inside the makeshift hut. The shelter had no walls or floors. A chill
crept in, eating its way under my clothes, around my
feet, into my bones. Rain splashed against my face. I had
never truly known the cold before, all my nerve end-
ings felt seared awake, dipped in ice. The smell of food
drifted over us, sweet and fragrant. My mother got up
and walked to the village houses. When she returned,

triumphant, she held an egg in her hands. "All they asked for was a ballpoint pen," she said. Salt, pepper, and herbs had been pushed in through a tiny opening in the shell, before the egg was boiled. It was the best thing I had ever tasted, the salt made my mouth water with pleasure. My mother didn't eat. She took a fragment of shell and traced a line against her wrist, over and over, until the shell disintegrated in her fingers. "Your father is in Phnom Penh," she said wistfully. "He'll be here soon. It isn't far. Along Route 1, it's just a hundred kilometres." I breathed in the scent of the wet ground, all the bodies around us, a rotting smell that expanded like moisture in my lungs. The stars crept near, too close, too cold. My brother held my hand. There was a low moaning of children, complaining, asking for food, that never seemed to cease.

I begged my father, Come and find us before we disappear.

One or two at a time, in the night, people went away.

Don't ask. Don't look into the holes.

Here is the answer: Do you want to see?

Every day, the quiet expanded. There were gangs of boys who came and went, who boasted of the cleansing they had done. They were sly and unpredictable, at sudden moments they smiled at us and the smiles were as sharp as tiny cuts. Angkar had divided us into the pure and the impure. On one side were the peasants, the *mulatan*, the true Khmer. On the other were the April 17 people, the population that had been expelled from the cities.

"The wheel of history is turning," Kosal said, lecturing us, his drooping eyes impervious to our hunger, to fear, to rage. "If you use your hands to try to stop the wheel, they will be caught in the spokes. If you use your feet to try to stop it, you will lose them too. There is no turning back."

He called us the new people, he said we must abandon our diseased selves, we had to cut loose our dreams, our impurities, our worldly attachments. To pray, to grieve the missing, to long for the old life, all these were forms of betrayal. Memory sickness, Kosal called it. An illness of the mind.

In the hut that night, the banker sighed for everyone to hear, "If I lose my mind, forget everything, became ignorant, will I be cured, Monsieur Angkar?" He stayed alone in a corner and nobody answered him. "You imagine," he whispered, looking at us, "that it will end. Don't you?"

Every day, we woke on a knife edge and we ran along it. We crushed *makloeu* berries and used the dark juice to dye our clothes. We cut our hair. When the sky was still black, the adults were summoned to their work brigades. From four in the morning until nightfall, they ploughed the soil, dug canals, planted seedlings, then transplanted these seedlings to the fields. Twice each day, Angkar rationed us a bowl of water with two or three spoonfuls of rice. My mother would eat quickly and then sit very still, holding her shivering body. "I'm tired, my darling," she told me. "I've never known such tiredness."

At first, we children were left behind. We scavenged the nearby forest and collected firewood, roots, fruit, and tree bark. My brother, who had never fit in with boys his own age, who preferred to sit at home with his records, had an instinct for the wild. With the dentist's son Oun, and a few of the village boys, he choked rabbits, twisted their necks, pulled them inside out. When we had meat, if for a moment I felt full, daylight seemed to expand again, colours returned and melted the tightness in my chest.

One of the *mulatan*, an old woman, tried to keep us occupied. She gave us seeds and spoke kindly about soil and water. She said the war had left Cambodia in disrepair. The Americans had bombed our schools, our roads and reservoirs. To survive, we had to feed our country. Food was our first defence, our most powerful weapon.

The seeds were like letters in my hands. Day after day, I knelt in the dirt, dragging weeds from the ground, imagining the beans, peppers, and cucumbers that would tangle around us.

"Feel my hands," my brother said one morning, nearly crying. "See how they're breaking." We were working together in the garden.

His hands were scratched and rough.

"You're imagining things," I told him. "They're just the same as always."

"If we had a gun," my brother said, "we could have all the food we wanted. If I had a rope . . ."

"Then what?"

Sopham wiped the sweat and tears from his face. After a moment, he said, "If Kosal could give you anything, what would you ask for?"

The sun was crawling up. In the fullness of a banana tree, I saw a figure reaching up into the leaves, trying to grasp the fruit, mistaking it for the sun. The picture, hallucinatory, swam in the air.

"Ask for something you can use," he said thoughtfully. "It's no good asking for the impossible."

But we had a home, I thought, a life. Why should we be ashamed? Kosal's world was the dream, I knew. Soon we would open our eyes and all of this would cease to be. I saw my father laughing, his stories like a page turning. I closed my eyes and willed him to keep walking, to come nearer.

I heard my brother's voice. "Ask to be a *mulatan*, and not one of us. The *mulatan* always have enough. They have food they can't even finish."

In small groups, the older children were sent away. The driver and his wife, the machinist and two of his boys, became sick and died. The students, the teachers, the banker, they vanished. If a family asked for a missing person, Kosal answered them by saying, "I don't know who you mean. I don't know this person." He had a cunning, dry expression in his eyes. He spoke slowly as if his words held threads of gold, he spoke softly and we had to lean in close to hear. "Why do you worry?" he would ask, a smile shading his face. "*At oy té.*"

One night, we were called to a meeting. Kosal stood before us. An old man, the hotel manager, knelt on the ground.

"Tell us," Kosal said.

I saw sweat gleaming on the man's face. He said, "What would you have me say, Teacher?"

"Tell us about your life."

The old man stared up, uncomprehending.

Beside them, the teenager, Prasith, carried a length of rope hung diagonally across his chest, worn like an ammunition belt. He handled the rope in his hands obsessively, fitfully, winding the end around one wrist, letting it fall slack, then taking it up again. The old man begged forgiveness. "You were happy then, weren't you?" Kosal said, interrupting him. "In the old society." There was a *tokoe*, a gecko on the wall clicking and clicking. "You think you're suffering now," Kosal said. He spoke as if he were feverish and light and faultless. "You think you understand, but what do you know about pain? I had to add everything together. There was a cost to your happiness." My mother tried to turn our faces away but Kosal rebuked her in his smooth, begging voice. He told us to pay attention, to learn from this man's example. He said that we must make ourselves strong and self-sufficient, we must never rely on anyone else, we must be clean inside because purity was strength. He said, "If your life brings us nothing, why should we not obliterate you?"

In front of us, the old man tried to crawl free. He swung his head away to shield himself, from Prasith and from all the watching eyes.

I wanted to block out the sound that his throat made, the panic in his hands. "Don't be afraid, *mit*," the teenager said, touching the old man's head, his face. "The earth is quiet. It will bring you quiet. Everything is only beginning again."

My mother came back with her eyes alight and her hands shaking. She had a plan, she told us. The time had come to run away. We were to be reunited with our father. "Phnom Penh," she said. "Norodom Boulevard. Of course he's there."

The world was upside down. I wanted to tell her there was no Phnom Penh, no Norodom, but it was like speaking to my father on those days when he couldn't hear us, his drinking had turned the volume down low. We were the sun going down, we were nothing but projections of light on the wall.

"Escape to where?" my brother said gently. "Escape to what?"

Feverish, my mother held her hands over her ears. Her body was both skeletal and swollen.

"He's been asking for you," she said. "Father has the plane tickets already. The flight. We'll go through Bangkok. See the water, see how it's receding?" She turned to me. "Terrible girl. Why do you blame your father? They sent him to study. They know his worth."

All night, my mother cried and twisted on the ground. Her legs were tender, bloated with water, she needed food, she needed vitamins, but all those things had vanished as if they'd never been. Kosal gave us medicine but the strange black pills dissolved on her tongue like charcoal.

"Ma," I whispered. "They're listening."

My brother stroked her hands. "She doesn't know us."

She lay between us, feverish, laughing.

The stars were everywhere. My father came and knocked at the door, repeating my name like an incantation. From room to room, I ran, turning my back on him. I walked through the hallways, I found the staircase that led to the rooftop. My father was there waiting for me. He held my hand and pulled me through a window and into a hidden space. He was covered in dust, it slid into the air, it coated everything. I lay my father down. There were pills everywhere, in his hands, tumbling out of his pockets, cascading down and skittering along the floor, *a thousand riels for a cupful*, I remember, a thousand riels, sometimes less. The boys playing kick sandal by the riverside, the cyclo drivers asleep in their vehicles. Endless colour and movement, a wonder before my eyes. "Are we going home now, Pak? I'm hungry and the moon is already out." His eyes were open. I filled this room with the names of books I remembered, I saw them on the thin, hard spines, floating on typeset pages, the texts of the *Tipitaka*, the Buddhist cannon, books by Alexandre Dumas, novels of Hak Chhay Hok and Khun Srun, I read their titles on clean sheets of paper that were rolled into the little typewriter my father had given me. My friends laughing when I had told them, puffed up like a tiger, that my father had given me this clattering machine, this grown-up beauty, something of my own.

"If I leave you," I asked him, "where will I go?"

"My sweet, you can never travel far enough."

Along the pitted road a truck came, churning up the ground with its thick tires. A beam of light advanced across the huts but I lay close to the earth, inside the darkness. Beside me, our friend, Oun, the dentist's son, was reciting verses in Pali, I could hear the running of sound: *There are trees bearing perpetual fruit, on these trees there are multitudes of birds. There also is heard the cry of peacocks and herons, and the melodious song of kokilas. There near the lake, the cry of birds who call, Live ye, Live ye. The birds roam the woods* . . . Passages he had memorized in school, just as we had done. Words pushed out of his mind, they floated down on us like air.

"My son, my son," his father said.

Oun's voice fell silent, he moaned as if trying to reel the sentences back in again.

His father said, "Angkar is listening."

There were spies, *chhlop*, everywhere. They came and waited in the darkness.

I fell asleep and became a small child again. I saw Wat Langka, its tiled rooftops, its rising eaves, stupas in the courtyard, the stone undulations of the Naga at the foot of the stairs. These were the forms that had coloured my earliest dreams. When my grandmother died, the monks had written her name on a slip of paper. They had set the words alight, watching the paper coil and burn, becoming ash inside a golden bowl. In the bright heat of morning, the monks' voices had risen through the air, arcing up against the temple walls.

All mortal things are impermanent, their nature is to arise and decay, having arisen they cease, in their stilling is happiness.

I opened the door to our apartment but nothing was visible. All the walls had been folded away.

"Tell me a story," my father said, his voice disembodied and sad. "My thoughts are dissolving. Don't turn away," he begged. "I was walking, the sky goes forever. Why is it changing to dust?"

I caressed his hands, I forced the pills between his lips.

—

The next morning, our mother could not stand. When Prasith came, we tried to tell him that she was ill and couldn't work, but the teenager just watched us with a faint smile on his lips. Kosal, he said importantly, had granted us permission to take our mother to an infirmary.

Prasith raised our mother up from the floor and carried her out of the hut. Her eyes flickered open and she tried to nudge him away. "Don't worry," he said. "Your children are here." Carefully, almost tenderly, he lay her inside a wooden cart. My brother and I took hold of opposite handles and began to push. Prasith led us away from the cooperative, his face tilted toward the clouds, as if luxuriating in the rising warmth. When our path joined another road, he gave us further directions and turned back.

"That boy," my mother mumbled, barely conscious. "I know that boy."

Nothing seemed real. The road we walked on was desolate and cratered and the sun never seemed to move, only to come steadily nearer, expanding into a dense fog. Twice, Khmer Rouge soldiers stopped us. They examined the permission slips Prasith had given us and then they waved us on, past workers who dissolved into the mist, past grey animals. Hours later, we arrived at the infirmary, a ruined concrete building where the nurses were only children and the sick lay everywhere on cots on the ground.

Upstairs, we found a place for our mother. There was no medical equipment but nurses came around with medicine, small white cubes that they stirred into bowls of water. Our mother was more alert now. She drank the medicine, her hands shaking, the water spilling. When the bowl was empty, she smiled weakly at us.

"Sugar," she said. "It's sugar."

Heavy rains began, lightning bursts, flooding. Hurriedly, we unrolled the bamboo blinds that clung to the ceiling. They were tattered and the wind swung them back and forth. We sat close to our mother, trying to keep her warm. I watched as she stared feverishly into my brother's face, looking for something, a detail beloved to her, a trace of someone I couldn't see. Sopham's eyes were like still ponds. I leaned my head against the wall, unable to rest.

Often, my father had gone away. He would return home, to Norodom Boulevard, with empty pockets and bloodshot eyes, he would say things like, "I got carried away. I started walking up Monivong and suddenly it was Tuesday but how that happened, I don't know."

"We don't know," my brother and I would echo. "We don't know!"

"All I remember," my father said once, his hands drifting limply in the air, "is looking up at the sky and thinking the sky would never go dark, it can't get dark because a hard blue lid covers everything. 'Whatever else we were intended to do, we are not intended to succeed,' who said that? A great man. A great, good man. We are not. We are not . . ."

For as long as I could remember, my father treated his sadness with Valium, pills he had begun taking when he was a student in Phnom Penh. I used to buy his medicine for him, by the cupful, in the Chinese market. But later, as the war dragged on, when the Khmer Rouge controlled the Mekong River and everyday the airport came under worse bombardment, the market ran out of pills. My father stopped sleeping, ate little, and worried constantly. The rockets and mortar fire cracked his nerves and sometimes his eyes seemed strange and elongated to me, bloodshot, red-rimmed, and lost. He wrote lists of names, people he could appeal to for money or support, people who could transport us to the border. He tucked the lists into my clothes for safekeeping.

One night, my mother set empty plates on the dinner table and looked searchingly at us, at him.

He ran his index finger across a plate, as if to check for dust.

"Would you like to go out?" he asked, flustered. His long body stooped toward her, like a fishing rod. I yearned to go to him, to pull him back. Our mother was not like other mothers, she had never been shy or decorous or restrained.

"Into the city?" my mother said, dropping her voice. "So we can dine with all these military men waiting for what, the end of the world? And the cost of rice, don't you realize?, it's up again and your wallet's empty. There's nothing here and tomorrow will be the same."

My brother watched, bright with embarrassment.

"Shhh," my father said, smiling weakly, eyes drifting to the window where voices rose like applause and touched the curtains, then dissipated back into the street below.

"Promise me, my love. We must get out. The war is ending but what does it mean?"

"I don't know. I'll get us out."

"At least Sopham," my mother said.

"I promise."

Downstairs, I saw people lying in streams of water, their mouths open, the rain leaking in. The floor was littered with bodies, and I couldn't differentiate the dying from the dead. There was no help for them. I hid upstairs, beside Sopham, unable to speak. Between us, the quiet had become habitual, we were wary of the spies and the *chhlop*, of saying the wrong thing. In Kosal's cooperative, a teenager named Milia had been caught keeping a diary. When the spies found it, Milia had disappeared. She never came back and I lay awake at night, staring at the place she used to sleep. It was occupied by another girl, as if Milia had never been. The diary, too, with all its thoughts and secrets, had been swallowed up. I dreamed they were under the huts, Milia, the banker, reaching their arms up, trying to help us.

The torrential rains stopped. One of the nurses saw that my mother was stronger, and we were discharged.

Walking home, my brother and I took turns pushing

the empty cart, our mother beside us, her steps tentative and weary. The sky was translucent, a watery gold that settled like steam over the distant fields. "Everything ends," my mother said. "But we're here. We're together, even if all else must fade away."

Prasith came to us. In our small patch of vegetables, he said, "Who owns all this?"

"Come and see," he said, calling the other children. "Whose food is this?"

I told him that this garden was ours.

Prasith got down on his hands and knees and began digging at the dirt. He snuck his fingers deep into a hole and extracted the tiny, misshapen root, a sweet potato, the earth still clinging to its wrinkled skin. "You don't understand," he said. "Not yet. But you will: we no longer steal from the people."

"I won't," I said.

"Steal," he whispered.

He put the tiny root in my hand.

Devotion softened his face. He said that people had suffered, they had given their lives to end this injustice. "That's why we fought this war," he said, "so that all of us might be free." He picked up a shovel that was lying nearby and began to dig, bringing up the roots and all the food. "I caught a boy stealing," Prasith said. "He took a watermelon but I punished him. Would you like to know how?"

The dry grass bit my feet. His voice suffocated me but I tried to close my ears, to cloak myself. Prasith stepped nearer, the words flowing out of him as if they were music.

"How brave you are," Sopham said, cutting him off. "You must be fearless to do a thing like that."

Prasith turned.

My brother stood beside me.

The boy's tone was mocking. "Are you?"

Sopham clasped his hands together. I willed him not to speak, not to show himself. "Yes," he said evenly. "I'm not afraid of my brothers."

Prasith stared, and then laughed. He held the shovel out. "Do your brother a favour," he said, "and finish our work."

Calmly, Sopham took the shovel and walked to the centre of our garden. I watched all the roots, all the seeds, come loose.

Prasith began trailing us across the fields. He would ramble excitedly. One moment sincere, the next, sly.

"If you want to be strong," he said one day, "you have to become someone else. You have to take a new name.

"For instance," he said, nodding at me, "you should take the name Mei."

I stared, bewildered. We had been up since dark, digging canals to irrigate the fields. In a little while, we would be called back to work. Six more hours of digging and shifting soil.

"*Mei, Mei*," he sang. The name, a common one, meant "lovely, beautiful." His eyes were half-closed, heavy-lidded. "See this?" He lifted his shirt to reveal an un-healed scar. "This is shrapnel."

My brother made a noise of disgust.

I averted my eyes.

"Shrapnel," Prasith repeated, watching me, letting his shirt fall.

My brother had glimpsed a frog and now he dropped to his hands and knees. The tall grass shifted around him.

"B-52s," Prasith said. "*Whomp-whomp-whomp*, like that, everywhere." He tilted his head back and stared at the sky as if it might fall down on us. "The light, it breaks. It breaks people open as if they're dogs or dirt. I looked up and there were no houses, no people. Just this hole."

Shyly, he bowed his head. "I'm important here. But, really, not even Kosal has any power. Me or him, it's like using an egg to break a stone."

I couldn't understand. "But who decides?"

Prasith smiled.

I persisted. "Who's the stone?"

"Too slow, too fast, here's the stone now." He swung a bit of rope in the air, laughing at me. "Here it comes. What can you do to stop it?"

My brother stood up. He held the frog by its dark, crooked legs and then swung it, hard, against a rock. "Too late," my brother said. "Too slow."

The animal in Sopham's hand convulsed.

I looked at it, sickened, starving. We could almost see through the frog's skin, to its lungs and guts. Slowly, pitifully, its feet beat against nothing. I turned away. To hide the trembling in my hands, I kept walking, kept moving. When I turned back to look for my brother, I saw Prasith's cooking fire, their two heads bowed together and white smoke that coursed into the sky.

I stood watching until they stood up, until they kicked the fire out.

That night, my brother showed me the treasure Prasith had given him. Two eggs, impossible things. We shared the first and gave the second to our mother. She ate it slowly, gratefully, her eyes closed, chewing the egg and then the shell itself. She told us that she had dreamed about our father. Pa had come with a knife, she said. He had cut us free.

Before we slept, my brother tied our wrists together, the way Prasith had taught him, so that if one of us were taken, the other would wake.

When Prasith restrained the boy, he didn't resist. This is the way my brother described it to me. The boy, Tao, the eldest son of the machinist, had stood there, motionless.

My brother stared at the ground. Prasith had given him new sandals to wear, and they felt heavy and unfamiliar to him, the rubber hot from the sun.

Calmly, Prasith took his own krama and tied it tightly around the boy's face. It choked Tao's breath and he stumbled and fell forward. Against his skin, the fabric of the krama grew dark with sweat or tears.

"Do you feel pity, Sopham?"

The air had become cold, Sopham told me. The sky, the colours, the feel of the air, the breath in his lungs, even the passing seconds were cold. My brother could feel the older boy watching him.

When Tao's mutilated body lay between them, Prasith cleaned his knife carefully in the grass.

"I used to think it was strange," Prasith said, "even terrible, but now I understand how it is." There was a shivering in his voice. "We have to let the sand wash away so that everything that remains will be clearer, stronger.

"No one will ever invade our country again. No more fighting, no more wars. Do you see? We're nothing but waterways. Nothing but drops of water." He was staring at Sopham so intensely, my brother had the sensation that the edges of his body were being sheared away.

"Your father was a translator, wasn't he?" Prasith said. "I think you went to Chatamukh School. Maybe there's some part of you that remembers me."

My brother studied the body, the soft creases of Tao's clothing. He said, "It's as if that time never was."

Prasith began undoing the rope that bound Tao's arms. They walked away, leaving the body where it was, folded over in the grass. "Look, this is what happens when people disappear," Prasith said. "*Bat kluon*. What will we do? All the bodies are fading away."

The seasons were changing, and all around me the harvest shone, brushed gold. I saw my brother and Prasith approaching from a distance. They walked confidently, arms relaxed, the rifle on Prasith's back angled to the sky. I was watching them when Kosal came and told me, proudly, that my name was on a list. I looked up at him, uncomprehending. "Come," he said, and I followed him behind the huts to where a line of girls was waiting.

He told me to stand with them.

I went to the end of the line.

Through the gap between the huts, I saw the pristine fields, strangely bright. My brother running toward me.

Kosal was speaking, addressing us. He said we had been chosen to join a children's brigade, we would travel south, we would serve Angkar. Around us, the cooperative seemed unnaturally loud.

"For how long?" I asked.

He looked at me, a pleasant expression on his face. "Oh, not long."

There were people now, shapes approaching. I looked up and saw Sopham. My entire body began to shake. I began walking away, in the direction of the huts, look- ing for my mother. Prasith was there, I had not seem him arrive, he took my hand and led me back. "Mei," he said. "Where are you going?"

He returned me to the end of the line. "Everyone has a place," he told me. "Everyone has a function."

Sopham and my mother were together now. She was there, she was holding me. "They want to take me away," I said. My mother's eyes were swollen, gleaming.

"Hush, my sweet," she said, caressing my face.

"Please, Ma."

"Hush, my girl," she said, her voice fading. "We have no choice." In her hands were the tin plate and spoon that she used. She folded them into my hands. "You'll come home soon. You must be brave."

"Ma," I begged. "Help me."

Gently, so gently I do not know if I imagined it, she pushed me away.

A lone cadre escorted us, single file, along the narrow ridges of the rice fields. We were a dozen hungry chil- dren, slipping in the mud, running to keep up. I saw tanks and rusted farm machines lying abandoned in the open. Grass slid through them, sticking up like hair, and I told myself that I would see these same objects when I came back again, in a few days, in a week or two. We walked until the sun was high, and we kept walking past crops that were a verdant green, their stalks blur- ring in the heat. I couldn't breathe, I felt my mother's fingers pushing against me. Red clay coated my feet and clothes. You have no possessions, no history, no parents, the cadre said. Your families have abandoned you. The sleeve of her shirt fell back, exposing her slender arms, the colour of wet wood. I thought of my mother gazing at Sopham, going from soldier to soldier, pleading for my father. Open your hands, the cadre said. Let go. If you are pure of heart, you have nothing to be afraid of. This is the revolution that is coming, that is here.

Rithy

opham had heard singing in the fields. This is the way he described it to me, later on, in the caves.

In the middle of a harvested field, he and Prasith had come to a *sala*, a meeting place, where a group of boys sat singing, a teenaged girl watching over them. When the song ended, Teacher called my brother forward. She asked his name.

"Rithy," he said.

"Can you add these numbers together, Rithy?"

"No."

"Can you read?"

"Some."

"What work did your father do?"

"He had a stand in the market. He sold palm sugar."

"How old are you?"

"Nine."

The questions kept coming but he answered them all, concealing himself like a stem overlaid with branches. His new name, Rithy, meant "strength." In Phnom Penh, in the temple schools, a new name had been a rite of passage, a bridge from one shore of life to the next, the symbol of a transformed existence. While Sopham answered questions, Prasith stood beside him, listening carefully, nodding as my brother spoke.

The noonday sun scorched the grass. "Fine," Teacher said at last, when all her questions were done. "You can stay."

Prasith left to return to Kosal's cooperative. Before they separated, he told my brother to be careful, that the spies were everywhere, Angkars climbing over Angkars. He said that, in our old cooperative, everyone, including our mother, was safer alone.

"She was relieved that you were leaving, wasn't she?" Prasith said. "Just like when your sister went away. Mei's school is just like this one."

He climbed onto his bicycle and pedalled slowly into the sky's orange haze.

Each morning, Teacher rounded them up to practise military drills: running, digging, hiding, loading their weapons, aiming, and firing. There was no ammunition, and sometimes the guns themselves were made of soft wood, newly carved and still smelling of the forest. The boys threw rocks at targets and screamed belligerently, cursing spies and agents and counter-revolutionaries. The Americans and the Vietnamese were pressing at the borders, Teacher said, and every child, every Cambodian, must defend their country. We are pure, she said, we are free within ourselves.

"Children become Masters," Teacher said. "The bread outgrows the basket."

They sang everyday. Later on, they sang when they carried out the punishments. Sopham had always had a beautiful voice. Before, our mother used to say that he sounded like In Yeng, and it had been In Yeng records that had crowded my brother's bedside in Phnom Penh. He used to approach the record player with a kind of earnest pleasure, resting his forehead against the wooden case when the music started. He didn't play kick sandal or *tot sai* with the gang of kids on our street. Those records had been like water to him. He drank and he drank, he was never satisfied.

They had songs to sing even if the words were foolish. Let us destroy the white and glorify the black! Let us dignify the unlettered and eradicate the learned! The judgments were foolish too, but the boys followed orders anyway, there was nothing to be gained in arguing. For them, plastic bags were weapons. Farm tools were weapons. He tried not to dirty his bare hands. Even up to the last moment, he told the guilty not to be afraid. My brother would walk back at night, across the fields, invisible even to himself. When morning came, the sky seemed a little less vivid, a shade lighter, but the shapes around him were clear, pristine.

He slept in a house with a dozen other boys and they ate rice everyday, there was meat sometimes and always vegetables. In the fields, they saw battalions of workers and they marvelled at the clumsiness of the city people who fell in the mud and broke the implements and injured the animals with their stupidity. Until now, he'd had no idea how vast these rice fields were, how much effort and waste and life were needed to feed a country as small and weak as his. There was too much water and there was too much sun. There were broken dams and flooded crops, there were crabs in the mud and shoddy seedlings. There were closed doors all over this country so farmers died without anyone noticing, they had died generation after generation, from starvation and swindling and finally bombs, until Angkar came and turned the world upside down.

"Your parents deceived you," Teacher said, "They told you to eat and drink, but how could you when your brother had nothing? When your sister was dying of thirst?"

No city, he thought, could ever be as beautiful as here. The tall stalks of swaying rice, golden brown. Families of sugar palms and coconut trees diminishing into the horizon.

Days passed when he endeavoured to be strong, uncorrupted. He was afraid to think too hard about the Centre, which people said existed in Phnom Penh, in the abandoned buildings beside the river. Angkar was all powerful. Angkar never slept because the Centre consisted of every one of them, watching and listening, reporting and punishing. Everywhere you are, there is the Centre.

Occasionally Prasith came on his bicycle and they walked together in the fields, using long sticks to prod the softest mangoes from the trees. The fruit always helped. He craved sugar and sweetness but against his will these things jogged old memories, dormant images like furniture in a pitch-black room. When Sopham asked about our mother, Prasith said she was the same, the very same. My brother asked if he could see her, but Prasith replied that it was impossible.

"The spies are watching your mother," he said. There was a new edge in Prasith's voice, the boy seemed older and more wary. "The new Angkar suspects everyone. Even Kosal has been arrested."

Sopham saw the bruises of a thousand eyes upon them.

"One day, you'll go east and defend the country," Prasith said, trying to reassure him. "We'll both go east. I would be proud to be a soldier."

My brother hoped that this was true. To fight an enemy, a real enemy, would be a relief. He took a breath and said the words he had prepared. "My mother used to tell us that you looked familiar to her."

Prasith's face was empty of expression. "My father and your father knew each other. I lived there, in Phnom Penh, but not for long." When he looked at Sopham, his eyes were calm, untroubled. "But they're ghosts now, aren't they?"

On the day Teacher told him that he had been chosen, my brother was happy but he didn't reveal it. What is

Sopham? he asked himself. He is a seed in the dirt, belonging to no one. Rithy will survive for a little while, and then he, too, will disintegrate. If only he could have counselled our father, my brother thought. Maybe this knowledge would have protected him; our father had not known how to cleave his soul.

Teacher told him that he had been selected to work in a security office. The office consisted of a small prison, run by a Khmer Rouge named Ta Chea, and it was housed in a concrete building that used to be a school. First, my brother was a guard and then, later, he was brought into the little rooms where the enemies were questioned. He was the youngest of all the interrogators and Chea told my brother that he should be proud. There are many prisons like ours, Chea said, all over the new country. The interrogators were pulling truth from the bleakest corners, they were the hands and the eyes of Angkar, they were the ones, the only ones, who refused deception. "Don't be afraid," Chea told him. "You have a strong character and an upright mind. They can't harm you." He said it was my brother's goodness that cut the prisoners, it was his honesty that sought the truth.

The prisoners arrived blindfolded and tied with rope. My brother studied them as each session began, chilled and fascinated. One night, Prasith arrived. My brother saw his friend helped down, gently, from a truck. His interrogator asked Prasith to give a biography and to name all the remaining members of his family. Then he had to repeat his life story, over and over. Kosal had betrayed Prasith before he died. The teenager was corrupt, Kosal had said, his only aim to sabotage the revolution. He had gone to school in Phnom Penh, his father had worked as a driver for the French Embassy. All this time, Prasith had kept this information hidden. During the bombings, the B-52s had spared almost no one in his village yet Prasith had somehow managed to survive. He was a traitor of the worst kind, an insect to be purged, a boy who had always put his own survival first. My brother knew this was true. Somehow, Prasith had never completely believed. Maybe Angkar was right, maybe the country had always been most vulnerable from within.

The dying always beg for water. In the prison, the interrogator's job is to trace all lines to the enemy, to lay bare the networks of connection, and then to follow this taint to every corner of the country. My brother was taught to do this methodically, calmly, without losing control. Chea kept track of the names that surfaced during each prisoner's interrogation. He noted them in a ledger, then he sent messages to the cooperative leaders: a sheet of white paper, folded four times, containing only names, a date, and the place of the summons.

Chea rotated the interrogators regularly. By the time my brother saw him, Prasith was already dying, his mind had come apart. He didn't recognize Sopham.

"You must do whatever is necessary," Chea said, turning the pages of Prasith's file. "You must make Prasith uncertain about the question of life and death, you must let him hope that he may survive."

Our mother had always spoken of the *pralung*, which is something like the idea of the soul. Sometimes, Sopham told me, the people who survived the longest in prison were the ones who had too great a *pralung*, too many souls, for it took so long to remove them. A body did not have to die, he learned, for the *pralung* to be damaged, to grow crooked, become wasted, to finally disappear. He saw people who never cried and people who wept continuously from the moment they entered the prison.

"Most beloved and respected Angkar," Prasith had said. "Most beloved. Most respected." His words were disjointed. "I swear to you on all that I love, I have never betrayed you. Please don't abandon me here. I swear to you, the enemies surround us."

My brother became familiar with the workings of the human body, with the tissue and the blood and the organs and the delicate, fragile forces that held a boy together. Cut this knot here, and the hand or the leg or the heart becomes useless. It was both mysterious and simple. Every day, my brother fought to banish all the unnecessary raging inside himself, to become as devoted and steadfast as Chea.

Before he died, Prasith told detailed, fantastic tales, he admitted freely to being a spy, he described America as a place where citizens lived on airplanes or underground, leaving the surface of the country empty as a sheet. The

CIA had recruited him at a young age, he said. They had sent him messages hidden inside pieces of clothing. They had signalled to him from the cockpits of their planes. The truest believers, he said, describing the agents he worked for, were the most indifferent monsters.

My brother became obsessed with water. His throat felt parched and rough, he hallucinated about water, he hoarded it in plastic bags and left these in the fields. Sometimes he stood and gazed at the shackled enemies and drank water in front of them as if to prove it was still there, it still existed within their reach. When it rained, he sat and watched the water moving over the ledges of the concrete building, seeping into the ground, falling and falling from the nothingness above. He watched it gathering in the clay jugs behind the building where the enemy was sometimes brought to be forced down under the clear, clean water. A blessing turned into a torture.

"I just went on with all the same things," he told me. "What did it matter if I believed or not? Ta Chea told me to think of him as my father. He said he would protect me as a father would."

In the prison, he let music run in his head. He thought about his hero, In Yeng, the singer, and wondered what had happened to those recording studios in Phnom Penh, to the television screens and singers, to the machines and microphones and boxes of records. Music, he knew, was recorded on to strips of brown tape, tape that spun around and around a metal reel. You could store music in canisters, you could lift it in stacks. If tomorrow the Khmer Rouge disappeared and he could return home, would he go? His collection of records might still be there but he knew that when he put his fingertips to the wooden case, when he set the needle against the grooves, the record might spin and spin and leave him wanting. Now the singer would be an executed man. Now all the reels of tape would have burned away and what joy was there to be had in such a return? My brother was nine years old. He had committed murders, he told me. He had tried to save himself and he had seen things that even our father, until the end of his life, could never have imagined.

A woman named Chanya came into the prison. They kept her for three weeks and, every night, she was interrogated. Her confession was nearly complete when Chea sent my brother to her. The woman was dying, on the table where she had been shackled, her arms and legs were impossibly thin. Her voice was so weak, he had to lean over her to catch the words.

"I'm hungry," she whispered.

"I have rice for you."

"Please. Just a spoonful. Please."

He gave her the rice, and then a sip of water.

"Thank you, my son. You are kind."

The next morning, before dawn, he found himself

seated beside her again. The gaps between her sentences had grown longer. He did not light the candle.

"You must tell him," she said. Her eyes stared up at the stained, dingy ceiling.

"Tell who?"

"Your father. Your brothers."

He hesitated, thinking. And then he said, "If only I could find them."

"They're in the caves."

"Which caves?"

"You know. The place your father hid when he fought the Americans. The men are waiting for you."

"No, I can't find the way by myself."

"But the map, my son. He drew it so carefully."

"They took it from me."

She breathed heavily. "What is that sound?"

It was the splashing of water in the buckets outside. "The children are washing in the river." A sad smile touched her lips. He was an instrument, he told himself, only an instrument. "After school today," he continued, "I stopped at the market. I bought you *kralan* from the lady with the curly hair and the gold tooth." He kept talking. The words seemed to soothe her. After a long time, she turned her head. "It's sweet," she said. "This *kralan*, still warm."

That evening, he was sent to her again. Her eyes were closed. He thought she was unconscious and he repeated her name. "Give me your hand," she said. He reached out and held her. Weakly, she ran her thumb over his fingers. "You've been chewing your fingernails again. Down to the quick. My poor Tooch. Always so nervous."

Between their hands, there were two small pieces of paper. They were rolled up, small as a stem, tucked into a gold ring that was so narrow, it could only have belonged to a child. He slid them free and opened them. On the first scrap, a map had been drawn. The paper had been folded so many times that the ink lines of mountains and jungle paths bled into the creases. "Poor little Tooch," she said, letting him go, turning her face away. "My poor boy."

She was taken from the prison that night and killed. Sopham locked himself in a storage room and used a candle to study the map. He could still hear the woman's breathing, the shallow exhalations. When he was small and learning to tie his first knot, our mother had told him that a rope almost never breaks within the knot itself. Instead a rope is weakest just outside the entrance to a knot, where the load is greatest. The map showed a way to the heavily guarded Vietnamese border, into the caves and out again. The second scrap of paper held a single phrase, written so lightly he almost didn't see it.

The river has flooded this year.

A smuggling ring, he thought. A code.

He returned to the map. If disciplined, perhaps he could travel there in a single day. My brother knew that Angkar would seek his family out, uncles and aunts, cousins, friends. They would be identified and arrested. He no longer believed that our mother was alive. Who was left? Only his sister. Only me.

When he could see the map in his mind's eye, my brother burned the papers. He placed the ashes on his tongue where they turned to paste and little by little dissolved.

He waited for the hot season to end. In the forest beyond the prison he hid lighters, clothing, uncooked rice, paper, pencils, candles, a good knife. Rithy existed and survived. He waited and kept his hands and his face impeccably clean but inside, there was someone else, a boy who watched, who had no need for language, who saw everything but never spoke, a boy who waited in the dirt for the end of one season and the start of another.

When news arrived at the prison that a girl at the reservoir was searching for Prasith, my brother, ever reliable, asked permission to bring her to the security office. He had done this before for other enemies. Chea, suspicious of everyone but my brother, agreed. Sopham hid his supplies on his body. He set off on an old bicycle, carrying the travel pass that Chea had given him.

❖

Every day, hauling mud in the bottom of a vast, dry reservoir, I followed Bopha's tracks. Our work unit, made up of three dozen girls, moved from project to project.

Sometimes we hauled mud or shit, or we dug with our bare hands, or we gathered wood. Sometimes we just marched from one destination to another, guided by a brutal but confused cadre. Bopha, Chan, Thida, Srei, Vanna, so many more, these are the children I remember. Oun, the dentist's son, arrived here, too, part of a children's mobile unit.

At night, I slept beside Bopha. We were the same age, we had the same blunt haircut, the same hollow bellies, but her eyes were bright and questioning and alive. Somehow, months of working in our brigade had not dulled them. When she laughed, she covered her eyes with her hands. All I would see was her upturned mouth, pale lips, a flash of teeth, stained fingers.

Every few weeks, Bopha would leave the reservoir at night. She would walk into the fields, through the blackness, until she reached the cooperative where her older sister lived. These nights were always the worst for me. My terror grew and grew, choking my breath. I wanted every noise, every approach, to be hers. Somehow, Bopha always succeeded in avoiding the patrols. When she returned before dawn, I held her more tightly, I watched her constantly, I did not want to let her disappear.

I recognized my mother everywhere, in the groups of women whose arms and legs were thin as blades, who dug endlessly at the ground. I tried to climb away into my mind, there were tunnels there, lakes, shelters within shelters. Memories came to me like objects sliding off a shelf. Week after week, I tried to convince myself to go back, just as Bopha did, but I kept putting it off. The darkness held a terror for me. Many times, I dreamed that I went home but my mother was already gone. No trace of her, no record, remained. Everything I knew had gone away. All around me, hour after hour, I heard the steady crack of shovels against earth.

At the height of the dry season, Oun beckoned to me across the reservoir. Briefly, a line connected us, taut for a moment, before he dropped his eyes. Slowly, cautiously, we drew nearer to each other, until we were side by side. Oun set his basket down, pretending to be occupied with it. "I went back," he said. "I saw my mother." I tried to shield my eyes from the glare of the sun. He hesitated, picking some rocks out of the basket. "Sopham was gone, sent away like us." One by one, the rocks came out. "I heard your mother was ill and that Angkar sent her to the infirmary." "Oun," I said. I saw the basket lifting, and then his bare feet, dark against the soil. The sun was nearly in the centre of the sky. It had taken him this long to reach me. "Do you know the place?" he asked me. His words came quickly now, rushing out. "It's where my father died. You must know it. In this sub-district, there's only the one infirmary."

I glimpsed a cadre walking toward us.

"I know it," I whispered.

Desperately, I pushed my hands into the warm mud, digging, busying myself. Time slowed. The morning light had solidified around us, holding each object, making every outline, all the shapes and all the people, precise unto themselves. I looked up. The cadre was watching us from a distance.

"Go," Oun said, moving away. "Don't wait."

I remember very little of the journey. Bopha gave me her sandals, which were newer than mine and in better condition, and then we went, moving through the impossible blackness, quickly, carefully. We had learned to be wary of injury. Wounds didn't heal anymore. In the heat and humidity, the smallest wounds could become infected. In the reservoir, people died from negligible things, a cut, a piece of rotten food, a single mistake made in a moment of exhaustion. As we ran, I saw Oun and the other children, I saw the cadre, Vuthy, who took care of us and who tried to be kind, but of Sopham or of my mother, my thoughts were bare. Not even their faces came to me. It was as if I could not lift them out from the darkness. We walked on and on, the night stretching around us.

At the edge of a road, Bopha took my hand. She was continuing on to see her sister, and we had agreed to meet back at the reservoir by morning. "Don't stay away too long," Bopha said before letting go. Within seconds, the shape of her had vanished into the emptiness.

People slept on straw mats or on the filthy tiled floor, with nothing to cover them or to keep the rats away. A girl wearing a long apron gave me a candle so that I could search for my mother. Slowly, I moved between the bodies, circling once, and then again, and again. I glimpsed a woman's loose clothing, her dark hair, and finally her face, childlike now, young again. My mother was so very thin, I had not recognized her.

There was no food in the infirmary. People lay covered in flies, too weak to climb out to use the latrine, unable to scavenge and feed themselves. They groaned and cried for water. My mother's hands were so tiny, they could fit inside my own. I stroked her hair and whispered her name. I said that her girl had come back, I had come to take her home. The wind blew inside and cooled us. A memory came to me of the sugar water she had drunk, perhaps a year ago now. It seemed like it must be a different girl, a different mother. She opened her eyes and looked at me as if from a great distance.

"Are we going home now?" she asked finally. *Yes*, I said. The lie felt bitter on my lips. "He's there," she said. "Father."

A boy came and said he was a doctor and he gave me a white paste to rub on my mother's chest. The paste was chalky and strange, it smelled of the earth and some herb I couldn't identify. She asked me where my brother was.

When I told her I didn't know she said, "He went away with that boy. They went away and then the boy came back alone."

Gently, I rubbed the paste onto her skin and as I did so, tears began to run from her eyes. I could not bear it. I blew the candle out.

The night passed slowly. The infirmary was never still. People called to ghosts who were not there, living ones or lost ones, names that no one answered to. The words filled the space like an incantation. Unable to sleep, I got up and went outside. First light came, I thought of Bopha waiting for me, and the mud of the reservoir seemed to grow brighter in my imagination, all the black-clothed workers, war slaves, the cadres sometimes called us, though the war had ended long ago. Here, in the infirmary, there were mothers and fathers and children, but hardly any who belonged to each other. Infrequently, the nurses came through. They were hardened now, more unforgiving than they had been before. I saw a woman being sent back to her work unit. Stone-faced, unable to weep, she left a bundle of food beside her son. Rice, fruit. By evening, the food had disappeared but the boy had not moved. I had hideous, nightmare dreams about my brother. On the third morning that I was there, I saw the nurses lift the boy's body and carry it away. All day, my mother did not open her eyes.

I scavenged, going farther and farther afield because the land near to the infirmary had been picked clean. In my mother's pocket, I had found her travel pass and I carried it everywhere with me. The pass was signed not by Kosal, but by a name I didn't recognize. I searched desperately for frogs, lizards, crickets, but my movements and my thoughts were slow. I, too, was starving. I returned with herbs and wild grasses and made a thin soup for us both. "The food is ready," my mother said. "Call your brother to the table. Give him a little rice." All too clearly, I could see the images in her mind, our white kitchen, her silvery pots, her family. I lay beside her and tried to disappear into my mother's world, to become her, to keep her near and lose myself instead. I begged her to be strong, to come back. I could not bear to survive alone.

On the third day, the boy, the doctor, came and told me that I had to leave. I asked who would take care of my mother and he said that he would. "Who will bring her food?" I asked. He said that Angkar would provide. I said that I would not leave, and he looked at me, surprised. He asked my name and my work unit. When I didn't

answer, he asked to see my travel pass. I showed him the
one I had taken from my mother. He stared at it for a
long time, and then he flung it back. He could not read,
I realized. The child doctors of the Khmer Rouge could
not even read. He told me to leave immediately, that she
was no longer my responsibility. I knelt on the ground,
weeping, trying to wipe the dirt from the scrap of paper.

My mother's chest rose and fell, struggling on and on.
A nurse came and told me, urgently, that I must leave,
all the relatives had to go, the doctor had sent word to
Angkar. And then what? I wanted to ask her. What more
could Angkar do to us? But the nurse had already hurried off. The world had grown too large for me, it was
asking too much, too much. I held my mother's hand,
I kissed her fingers. "The rice," she said. "Please, my
darling. Bring me a little rice." The things I had scavenged lay around us. Fruit, herbs, water. I searched my
mind for what I should do, where I could find food, how I
could help her, but my thoughts felt like grains of sand,
scratching, tumbling. My father's stories came back to
me, all the heroes that persisted in Khmer poems and
myths, so many stories that promised us we were braver
than we were. I wanted to shake him, I wanted to tell him
that the things we try so hard to keep, the beloved, most
precious things, keep slipping through. We had always
been powerless to keep them safe. I got to my feet, I went

outside for air, and then I kept walking, kept going. At the junction where Bopha had parted from me, I stood, weeping, trying to will myself to return. Go back, I told myself. She needs you. She'll die without you.

I kept going, as if we were again leaving the city, this exodus that had begun and had never ended. I walked and saw the crowd beside me. People had carried the things they treasured, a machinist carried his tools, a grocer pushed a cart of groceries, my father carried books. In my mother's bag were photo albums, our clothes, our toys. Later on, all these things had been abandoned, bit by bit, on the side of the road. A space grew around me, it rose from the soil, a space in which there were no doors, no light or darkness, no landmarks. No future, no past. The things I had kept hidden from Angkar had not been buried deep enough. From far away, I saw myself as I had been many years ago, carried by my father. He swung me down and laid me in my mother's arms. I carried this image with me as I walked away, pushing it down, clothing it in darkness. Turning so completely away from it, the image slowly disappeared.

When I reached the reservoir, it was dawn. Bopha was awake, waiting for me. My thoughts, my memories, my body, were separating but she held me tightly, she tried to keep me from coming apart. She told me to go to Vuthy right away, to tell him I had been sick and I had gone into the forest to find medicine. That I had been feverish and had gotten lost but, this morning, I had found my way free again. I did everything just as she told me. In his hut, Vuthy watched me intently. When I had finished explaining, he told me to sit down. He gave me a plate of food with rice and fish, and when I was done eating he told me not to tell anyone about the food, to go back to my work unit, and to continue on.

The hot season ended. I lived and worked and dreamed beside Bopha. At night, while I listened, she spun stories for me. She told me about a boy named Chantou who had run away into the forest. "He lived up in the trees," Bopha said, "safe from the wild animals." She said that, in the north, the Tonle Sap floods everything, the lake rises so high it covers not only the buildings but the highest branches of the forest. In the trees, the boy Chantou had gathered up the dead bodies of sodden birds. He had found fish in the branches, stranded there when the water subsided.

"Fish in the trees," I said.

Bopha looked up at the starlight. "More and more the farther he climbed."

We imagined the boy Chantou. He lay beside us, telling his stories. Our own lives were littered with traps, unanswerable questions, and it was Bopha who first taught me how to escape from myself in this way, disappearing into the souls of other people, both the real and the imaginary.

Early mornings, in the forest beyond the reservoir, we tried to find food. We stripped bark from the trees, and then we put these curling strips into the puddles of water that had gathered in the indentations of rocks, and we drank the liquid up. Small birds came and hung upside down, warming themselves in the patches of light. When I stretched out my hands to capture them, they blurred away. We ate leaves, husks, stems, and wild grasses, but our stomachs couldn't digest them and it took too much energy to grind the food into pulp. I imagined climbing up into the highest branches and glimpsing the airplanes that had once paraded across the sky. Thida disappeared, then Chan, then Srei. Other children arrived to replace them. Su, Leakhena, Dara, every one of us like water spilling into the ground. My body was wearing out. I was so thirsty I wanted to pour the blue sky into the palm of my hands, swallow it in great gulps. One night, I remember, Bopha killed a snake and we charred it on the fire. The meat was leathery, rich, and tough. Bopha's face, her enormous eyes, lit up with pleasure.

My friend was wasting away. In my arms, Bopha seemed as insubstantial as the dry grass, as if the sea inside her had evaporated. "There's an answer to everything," she said one night when she was ill. "My grandmother told me, it's all written in a big book. I used to think that, one day, I would read it. I would walk into a temple, it would be as vast and rich as a palace, I would turn all the pages, I would see everything that had ever happened, everything that was coming."

She looked at me as if she could see straight into my heart, into the centre of who I was. "But I know now," she said softly. "I've looked and I've looked, but there's no answer for me."

I wanted to hear her laugh. I mimicked the pouting mouth of Vuthy, the way he bit his lip, the way every time he said the word *Angkar* he sniffed as if he had a cold. I held her hand and kissed her repeatedly, fearfully.

She told me that after they had been evacuated from Phnom Penh, a foreboding had come to her mother. Bopha's father had already been taken away, and her mother knew that Angkar had marked them. She believed that, unless her children rid themselves of their history, they would never be safe. One night, she packed their things and she sent both her daughters, Bopha and Rajana, away, one to the north and the other to the south. When you reach a camp, she said, tell them you're an orphan. Tell them your parents have died and you have no place to go. A few weeks later, Bopha said, her mother had been taken away and killed.

I remember birds sliding upwards into the ruby night. Once, while gathering kindling in the forest, I saw a tiger stalking a deer. I stood very still, thinking of my mother, believing that she had come now, she had forgiven me. Instead, the tiger vanished and the deer with him. They were the most beautiful creatures I had ever seen in the world. For Bopha, I gathered lime-green berries in a jacket of dew. But nothing I did could save her. Bopha died. Vuthy came, he helped me bury her at the edge of the reservoir, in a place where still leaves would shade her from the heat. Against her chest, in the pocket of her clothes, lay a picture of her sister, Rajana. Afterwards, fearful that Angkar would see my pain, I hid inside the forest. I asked myself how I had disappeared and why I could not remember the moment, the act. Was this the emptiness at the centre of creation, the nothingness to which I aspired? Was this the highest truth of all? I saw that I had not understood before, how deep, how wide, loneliness could be.

Hunger was erasing my being. Soon, I, too, would find my way into the trees. I went to Vuthy again. I told him I wished to find my brother, and I asked him to send a message to Prasith, a Khmer Rouge cadre. I gave him the name of our old cooperative. Vuthy looked at me, there was pity in his eyes. He said that he would do his best. I wanted to ask Vuthy what he had been before, what lives he had lived, I wanted to know how it was possible to be something more than what I was.

I continued to work in the reservoir. Chantou kept me company, returning to me night after night. My hands, my body, remained in the world, but slowly I released myself into the quiet grief of my thoughts.

Who lied to us? Chantou asked me. I tried to answer him, I tried to know. Maybe it was the ones who said we were living in a new age, a year zero, who said we must be strong, that purity was strength. I wanted to ask Angkar, How can we save ourselves and still begin again, how can we keep one piece and abandon all the rest? The devastation always moves inward, even to the last and highest rooms.

In the reservoir, the rains kept on. I thought another birthday must have passed and I was now eleven years old. No existence is permanent, I told myself. I held fast to the belief that all times, all wars, must come to an end.

Everything passes, my mother whispered.

Even love. Even grief.

Near the end of the rainy season, my brother arrived at the reservoir. I had been summoned to Vuthy's hut. My brother looked at me, held my eyes, then turned away.

"I need your signature, *mit*," my brother said to Vuthy. The cadre lifted the page. He studied it for a long time, then he turned to me, as if he had a question only I could answer. At last, Vuthy picked up a pen and signed the page. My brother unloaded a sack of rice from the bicycle and laid it on a nearby table. The cadre examined it, surprised.

The tires needed air and when I climbed on, we sub-sided even farther. As Vuthy watched Sopham began to pedal, navigating us down the muddy road, away from the reservoir. I sat on the seat and my brother stood and pedalled, the cotton of his shirt blowing out behind him, touching my face, my neck and shoulders. The coarseness of his shirt rubbed against me. I had dreamed of seeing him too many times, wished for it, imagined it. In the same moment, I believed and disbelieved.

When the cooperative was far behind us, he manoeuvred the bicycle to the side of a fast-moving stream. He took my hand and helped me into the water and he used my filthy clothes to scrub the mud and dried, old blood from my skin. I could not remember where the blood had come from. He rubbed hard and the clothes, so old and thin, began to disintegrate. The water was sun-drenched, it smelled of black dirt. "Are you all right?" he asked me.

I said that I was cold, only cold.

My brother nodded. "Look," he said. "I brought new clothes for you."

Nothing was what it seemed. Somehow he had grown taller than me, heavier. I put the clothes on. Emotion flickered behind his eyes, never quite coming to the surface.

"How did you find me?" I asked him.

"You sent word. Through Prasith. Do you remember?"

I nodded. He turned away from me and climbed back onto the bicycle, waiting. "And Ma," I said, trying to begin, but the words only slid away from us, unfinished.

"She's gone," he said simply.

In his voice, all the feeling had hardened and closed off.

It started to rain. The landscape turned murky, the road began to wash away from under us, but we continued on, hurrying west then south then west again, mostly pushing or carrying the bike over the dislodged road. Shadowy forms moved against the twilight, human beings freezing into trees, trees elbowing into human shapes. We stopped to rest and I opened my mouth and drank the rain.

When it grew too dark to see, we hid in a grove of trees and took turns sleeping. I woke to the sound of my brother reloading the AK, cleaning the barrel and the grip. He had a killed a creature while I slept, skinned it, and hung the flesh from a branch. The mosquitoes and flies surrounded it, ecstatic, and he took the meat down and wrapped it in leaves. We kept going.

Eventually, my brother turned onto a narrow track. We abandoned the bicycle in the mud. Slowly the ground gave way to jungle. I saw thick vines choking the gnarled trees, I saw frantic ground squirrels, enormous, furry insects with wavering antennae and burning eyes. We ascended and the mist rose with us, and then past us. On and on we went, climbing higher and higher. Daybreak came. We stopped only twice, sharing the rice Sopham had brought. Afternoon and then evening fell. The last light pebbled over the jungle floor, my brother moved faster and faster. I struggled to keep up. And then, in the gloom, we saw it at the same time, a crevice cut into the rocks.

Sopham held his AK in both hands. He went in first and then, when he had disappeared, I followed.

Nothing was visible. The cave smelled like a world condensed, all the earth and trees and rocks crushed to a handful of minerals. Sopham rustled in his clothing. Light flickered between us. I saw a match in his hands, and then a candle, thick and honey-coloured, the kind used for temple offerings. For a moment, Sopham looked at me, his eyes pale in the sudden light, and tried to smile. I saw my father's face, his disbelief, his masked sadness.

Deeper inside the cave, we rested. In a sort of grotto in the wall were the ends of other candles, a disintegrating scarf, burned-down sticks of incense, dulled bullet casings. My brother told me about the prisons, about Prasith, about the woman named Chanya. His voice was flat. "The good and the pure break," he said. "They always break." I remember water dripping endlessly down the cave walls. My brother went away somewhere, he started a fire, cooked the meat, and brought it back to me. He showed me the treasure he had kept all this time, the key to our apartment on Norodom Boulevard, in Phnom Penh. He asked me to take care of it, to keep it safe. We could not bring ourselves to speak about our mother. For a long time, while Sopham slept, I ran my fingers over the key, listening to my brother's breathing, his exhaled words. I told myself that I could protect him. The love I felt for him was like air, everywhere inside me, pushing me on.

Turn by turn, we passed through the long waist of the mountains, not knowing if we were deep inside the caves or almost through, not knowing if the border to Vietnam was near or distant. The groundwater rose to our hips and then subsided, draining away.

Sometimes the ceiling dropped low and we had to crawl forward, holding our mouths above the water, the AK lifted up. The farther we went, the slower our movements seemed, the slower my blood pulsed. At the end of a long passage, the cave flowered open into a grandiose space, hourglass columns, glimmering pools, still reflections. Light rained in through pinches and seams. My brother said that this was the place, Chanya's map would not lead us any farther. We sat against a wall, listening to the bats and the falling water. It felt like days passed, but perhaps it was only hours. I no longer know. We slept and woke, slept again.

I heard the crank of an AK. My eyes flicked open.

A man stood in front of us, a tall, thin shadow, appearing as if he had melted from the walls. There were noises behind him, a woman's nervous warning, and then footsteps, quickly retreating. Beside me, my brother woke. He lifted his hands, the palms facing out.

"*Mit*," Sopham said. The word echoed off the walls.

The man cut him off. "What district?"

"Peam Ro district, Prey Veng province."

The rifle edged nearer.

My brother's voice was trembling. "The river has flooded this year," he said.

Surprise showed in the man's eyes, and then it was gone. "Has it, child?"

"Yes, *mit*. The river has flooded this year."

"*At oy té*," he said softly, ambiguously. "Let it flood."

He crouched down in front of us, the gun supported on his hip, and studied our faces. His skin was faded, tinged grey. "Let's have the truth. Who are you, really?"

When neither of us answered, the man pushed the tip of the rifle against my brother's heart. "Hurry up," the man said. "Time is running down."

"Our friend showed us the way," Sopham said finally. "He had a map."

"I see. Where is this friend?"

"He was ill, *mit*. He died on the road. I'm sorry, he didn't −" my brother tried to say more but the words stuck in his throat.

The man lifted the barrel of his gun, rapping it twice against Sopham's AK. It was still strapped to my brother's body but now, carefully, he slid it free. The man took it. "Stand up," he said. He searched my brother and then me, his hands moving roughly down my arms, my jutting ribs. "Please," I said. "We have nothing."

He paused and stepped back. "If you have nothing, what should I do with you? What good are you to me?"

"All we want is to leave."

"Do you think it's so simple?"

I looked into his eyes, unable to answer.

A long time passed and Sopham and I lay together on the ground. The man watched us intently. Later on, people came. I saw a teenager wearing a belt of ammunition and, behind him, a woman carrying a baby. Her breathing was shallow, as if they had climbed far to reach this place. They sat down opposite us. Once, the baby came loose from her mother's arms. She crawled to me, pulled my hair, touched my face with her warm, bird-like hands. "No, baby," the woman said. Her baby made a happy sound, like a cat licking milk, and the woman looked at me with sadness and wonder.

The teenaged boy went away and then returned; I heard the scratch of his footsteps.

It was no longer possible to track the sun, to identify the hours, the nights.

My brother woke in a panic. "Feel my hands," he mumbled. "See how thin they are?" I held them. "No," I said, easing him back to sleep. "No." The baby in the woman's arm was snoring lightly. I fought to stay awake. "You have to deal with them," someone said. "Yes. The risk is too great." "They're harmless," the woman said. Someone grunted in dismissal. "But the others —" "The others are not coming." "We can't wait. They'll have to go separately." The name Chanya touched the air, but maybe it was only my brother's dreams seeping into me. I heard the dull clicking of bats, small pips, the beat of tiny wings.

"Please, *luk*," I said. The term of respect came back without my realizing. He looked up, startled.

"*At oy té.*"

"Don't leave us behind."

"No one will get left behind."

"You're frightening me," I whispered.

Ignoring me, he opened his krama and removed some crabs and a handful of rice. He offered this food to the woman and the teenager. They began to eat. The woman took a portion from what she had and brought it to us. In my mouth, the little crabs had serrated edges, it hurt to chew, but I could feel the blood flowing in me again, a quickened pulsing.

When the food was gone, they rose to their feet.

"Come," the man said, turning to us, his expression lost in the shadows. "It's time to leave."

We stood. My brother began washing his face in the water that slid along the walls, and then I, too, did the same. In his eyes I saw my own fear, my own acceptance.

The man walked first, and then the woman, myself, Sopham, and the teenaged boy. Every moment, I expected to hear voices, the release of the safety, the word *Angkar*. Instead, I smelled the sweetness of leaves, of roots, of the wet earth. The man disappeared through a narrow mouth of the cave walls. On the other side, I saw a soldier in army fatigues holding a green helmet in his hands. Without speaking, the soldier hid us in a nearby truck, underneath sacks of rice. The teenaged boy didn't come with us, he faded back into the opening of the cave. The truck shuddered into life, time seemed to contract and expand. I pulled one of the bags open, fed the grains into my mouth, held them there until they disintegrated. I willed myself to feel nothing, neither fear nor hope, only the jolting road beneath us, the weight of the burlap sacks. Twice, the vehicle was stopped. Both times, I heard men speaking Vietnamese, low voices followed by gaps of silence. Nobody searched the truck. We continued on.

Finally, the sacks were removed and what I saw seemed impossible, the night sky and a thousand stars burning. The woman and the child were bundled away down another road. "Are you ready?" the man asked us. We didn't know what to say, who to believe. "It's time for us to leave," he said. The soldier gave us biscuits, noodles, dried fish, a few cans of milk, and water, and then we climbed into a small wooden boat. It ferried us to another boat that waited, anchored in the sea. Inside was a shallow cargo hold filled with many people, many families, who watched us descend, their faces etched with fear. The man spoke to them in Vietnamese. He told us that these people had been waiting several days; already, they were running out of water.

We took turns lying down, first my brother and I, then the man, who told us to call him Meng. Above us, slats of wood had been removed and we could see up into the sky.

My last image of Cambodia was of darkness, it was the sound of nearly forty mute wanderers, of silent prayers. I closed my eyes. My father told me how Hanuman had crossed the ocean, how he had gone into another life. Look back, my mother said, one last time. I followed her through our twilit apartment, walked in the shade of my father, past bare walls and open windows, the noise of the street pouring in. Between us, she said, I had known love, I had lived a childhood that might sustain me. I remembered beauty. Long ago, it had not seemed necessary to note its presence, to memorize it, to set the dogs out at the perimeter. I felt her in the persistent drumming of water against the boat's hull. Guard the ones you love, she told me. Carry us with you into the next life.

Exhausted, holding tight to my brother, we set out across the sea.

Our time in the boat was infinite. One long night that battered on and on until the food was gone and the water drained away. Meng, ever watchful, would take my hands. Gently, he would massage my fingers and my cupped palms, telling me that soon, any day now, we would arrive.

He showed us a photo of a smiling man in an over-sized floral shirt and dark slacks. This was his younger brother, Sann. They had hidden in the caves together and then his brother had gone ahead with his wife and sons, using the same smugglers, arriving finally off the coast of Malaysia. The smugglers had given Meng this photograph. "To reassure me," Meng said, "and to raise the price."

"Do you come from the city?" I asked him, trying to see Phnom Penh, to hold it once more in my mind's eye.

"I was born there," he said. "But I lived many lives. Teacher, farmer, soldier."

"Khmer Rouge?"

He nodded. After a moment, he said, "Your father, what work did he do?"

"He was a translator. Angkar took him away." I didn't know how to continue. Hearing the words, I felt defence-less, ashamed. Meng lowered his eyes. Even here, in the crowded boat, he tried to shelter us, to give us space to breathe.

I curled on my side and watched my brother sleep. All the time he asked for water. "There is the tap," he said, half-dreaming. "But look, nothing comes out. I twisted it all the way around but there's no water, no water anywhere."

That morning, Meng paid the fishermen and they let us up into the open air. Sopham and I climbed out of the hold, clinging to the sides of the boat. We were impossibly small. The waves crowded against our ears, muting our thoughts. All was blue, all was noise.

"I saw so many things," Sopham told me. "One day, I promise, I'll find a way to tell you everything."

On the sea, we moved through a turbulent world, forever adrift. Three or four nights passed, but each day, no land appeared on the horizon. On and on we went until the night when the men came. The collision hit like an explosion. Once, these men had been fishermen, but now they were something else, some instinct that has no pity, no name. They robbed us, and then they forced the girls up out of the cargo hold. I remember the sound of crying, a noise like a serrated edge. Minutes passed, hours. I remember crawling between the bodies to the edge of the deck, away from the smell of fuel, but still the men were there. Pulling us back, taunting us. Time stopped. I have no words for what was done. Sopham appeared and we fell into the sea. I fell, I kept falling, and then my body rose to the surface. Still they were behind me, holding me, crossing oceans and continents. Coming into every room, every place, preceding me into my life. I no longer wanted to breathe the air. My brother kept repeating my name. He used his krama to tie my wrist to a piece of floating wood, checking and rechecking the knot. Don't leave me, I said. The boat withered and dark shapes bent across the water. I tasted salt, dreamed salt. Morning came and it seemed that we were caught on broken glass, countless fragments that turned the light aside. My brother said the guard had gone to sleep, he could go past, he could leave without her waking. I told him that our wandering was over, we had nothing more to be afraid of. The key was gone. I said that I could not bear to be alone. My brother wept. I was not strong enough to hold him. He opened his hands and I watched as the ocean breathed him in.

I saw my wrist and my hand bound to the wood but I no longer recognized it as my own. The knot my brother had tied would not come loose. Inside me, all the feeling went away.

❖

I can taste the faint, distilled light, it rests on my tongue like a coin. I am nearly at the edge of the city. The road gives way to open space, untrodden snow. The northern reach of Boulevard St-Laurent comes to an end and I stand at last at the river. Behind me, trees tower up into the pale sky.

On a park bench, a woman wearing ski gloves is carving letters into the wood. I can hear the hard edges of her blade, like an animal burrowing into the frozen ground. I remember how, in the ocean, the water had become a shining mirror, how the sun had touched everything and left no shade, no chasms. The fishermen who drew me from the water hurried across the sea until, finally, their boat reached land. I remember the sudden, incomprehensible, stillness. One of the men lifted me from the boat and I looked up and saw the high palms, the amber sky. The man who carried me began speaking, words that rustled together, and then I was passed into another person's arms. They brought me into a house where I was laid down and washed and covered.

Something has turned over in me, broken and come undone. I take my phone and begin dialling Meng's number. He picks up on the first ring. When he hears my voice, he shouts in joyful surprise. "It's Mei," he says to someone, to us both. "It's Mei!"

Voices rattle behind him. Grandchildren, he tells me, laughing proudly when I ask. "*Mes petits canards*," he calls them. One by one, they come to the phone and greet me in high-pitched voices, then my friend returns.

"Meng," I say finally. "On the boat that night, did you hear them coming?"

In all these years we've stayed in touch, I've never been able to talk about what happened. He, too, had been pulled from the water and saved. He asks me where I am. I tell him I am at the river, I have walked as far as I can away from the city, I cannot find a way to go any farther.

"No," he says. His voice is quiet. "I didn't hear them. Until the very last moment. I never heard them."

I want to tell Meng that I know too much, I have too many selves and they no longer fit together. I need to know how it is possible to be strong enough. How can a person ever learn to be brave?

"Janie," he says. "My child." He says that my parents, my brother, lived their lives. "They wouldn't want you to fight on and on. To fight even when it's done." Long ago, Meng and I had stood together at the water's edge. "Your daughter is leaving now," he had said, addressing my ghosts. "Your sister has found a new home. You, too, must walk to your own destiny." The incense in my hands had left its smoke in the air. The next day I would depart for Canada.

"We have to try again," he says. "Not just once but many times, throughout our lives."

I feel as if I am swaying over the river, but that this river, finally, is blind to me. I can see it now for what it is, only a membrane, a way down. *Leave me*, I think. *Let me go*.

Kiri

❖

Down in the subway, the tiled walls begin to shudder. A train storms in, coats flap backwards, a little girl's golden hair blows wild. One by one, we find seats inside the nearly empty cars.

I take out my phone again but there's no signal. Meng's words circle in my head, the train hurries through long tunnels, emerging into stations. We move from brightness into a furtive grey, my reflection floats against the window. "*Entre chien et loup*," Hiroji would have said. It was his favourite expression: that quality of light when we confuse the dog and the wolf, the beloved and the feared.

I was a graduate student when I heard him lecture for the first time.

On that day, I had arrived early to class. The visiting professor, dressed in a pinstriped shirt and pressed trousers, laid an image on the overhead projector. I recognized it from Lena's books, an ink drawing by Ramón y Cajal depicting a single neuron, a deep pool fed by, and feeding, dozens of arterial streams.

Students shifted papers, slept, took off their shoes, and daydreamed, but I was transfixed. The ebb and flow of Hiroji's voice, its polite refinement, its insistence, caught all my attention.

Partway through his talk, Hiroji described the experience of a woman who suffered from asomatognosia: for varying periods of time, she ceased to feel her body or its boundaries. All sensation — air on her skin, warmth, cold, the weight of her hands — vanished. Her thoughts continued, anchored to nothing. She herself was immaterial.

"She had lost her body," he told us, "but not her being.

"Let us take the example of Zasetsky," he continued, "a university student, a young man, shot in the head. But he survived." The bullet had cut a path through the parietal and occipital lobes of his brain, affecting Zasetsky's vision, movement, language, and sensory perception. His world was constantly shattering apart.

Hiroji laid a second image on the projector: a notebook page, crammed with sentences.

Zasetsky's physician, Aleksandr Luria, was, Hiroji said, one of the first to write the narratives of his patients. Luria treated Zasetsky for more than thirty years, finally collaborating with him on a medical text. Zasetsky wrote more than three thousand pages over the course of two decades, pages that he himself could barely read. Each sentence required that he hunt through the disintegrated rooms of his memory, fumble blindly for words, the simplest words, hoarding them like gold dust until he had enough to construct a sentence. An entire day would pass in which Zasetsky underwent a superhuman struggle to remember language itself; he might, if lucky, emerge from the effort with two or three sentences. Luria had hoped that, through this text, Zasetsky would not only remember his life, but he would make a wholeness of it. Neurologically, Hiroji said, it was possible for the world outside to fragment, to splinter, and yet for the self to remain intact.

"This writing is my only way of thinking," Zasetsky wrote. "If I shut these notebooks, give it up, I'll be right back in the desert, in that 'know-nothing' world of emptiness and amnesia."

After his lecture, in response to a question, Hiroji described the work he had done on the Thai–Cambodian border in the late 1970s, in the refugee camps. He went, he said, because his brother had been a part of the Red Cross humanitarian mission in Phnom Penh, Cambodia, during the years of the Vietnam War.

As the students filed out, I approached him. Awkwardly, I planted myself in his path as he made his way up the steep steps of the lecture hall.

He looked at me inquiringly.

"Excuse me, Professor," I said, staring at his shoulder. "Could I ask you, your brother, the one you mentioned, could I ask if he has returned to Cambodia and how he has found it there, for the people, and what is Phnom Penh like? This is something I've been wondering. Have they repaired the buildings and are people able to return to their former homes? Can you tell me, please, what the city is like?"

He stared at me, as if trying to translate my words into another, more decipherable, language.

"Oh," he said at last. "But he didn't come home."

I stared harder at his shoulder.

"What I mean is," Hiroji said, "my brother is still missing. James disappeared. In 1975."

"Oh," I said, blushing. "I see."

"But I went there. I went to Phnom Penh."

When I met his eyes, it seemed he was about to ask me something in return but I backed away from him, turned, and ran away up the stairs. The teaching assistant, standing beside Hiroji, called my name but I kept going.

Years later, when I met Hiroji again at the BRC, he still remembered this encounter. We were in my lab, the computer crunching its way through layers of statistical analysis, when he reminded me of it. I asked Hiroji to tell me about the border camps and the boy, Nuong, he had grown close to.

By then, something in me was changing. My brother was returning to me, so finely, so clearly, just as he had been at the end. I wanted to keep him near to me and yet, I told Hiroji, I couldn't live with this memory. There was nothing about his last moments that I could change.

Beside us, my computer scrolled through data, pulsing signals.

For hours we talked, roaming together, stopping at the wide branches of Gödel and Luria, the winter stillness of Heisenberg, the exactitude of Ramón y Cajal. He told me about memory theatres, how the Italian philosopher Camillo constructed his own in the seventeenth century. His theatre was a room filled with ornaments and images, inside a structure that he believed echoed the layout of the universe. Standing in this room, one could be simultaneously in the present and within the timelines of the past. Bopha's imaginary book came back to me, but now her book was something that I could enter. The pages would remain, like a library, like a city, holding the things I needed to keep but that I could not live with. If such a library, a memory theatre, existed, I could be both who I was and who I had come to be. I could be a mother and a daughter, a separated child, an adult with dreams of my own. These ideas, these metaphors and possibilities, were the gifts Hiroji gave me.

Once, I asked him, "Why are you so kind to me?"

Hiroji had looked at me with a gentleness that I will always remember. "Because you're my friend, Janie. Because a friend can do no more."

The doors of the metro clank open. This is my stop. We go up and up to the world above. On the sidewalk, snowplows come, flashing lights, slowing traffic.

Sunlight angles off the snow, blinding everyone.

On the fourth floor of the BRC, I go to Morrin's office. When he looks up, his eyes register surprise. I comb my fingers through my hair and tell him that I was delayed this morning. "Janie," he says, focusing on me. "Do you want to come in and talk? I've been thinking about you since –"

Alarmed, I step backwards. I ask if the talk can wait, I have some work to finish. He nods. The door rattles as I pull it closed.

Outside the door to my lab, I telephone Navin. When I apologize for not seeing them this morning, he says, "Why don't we visit you in the lab? I was planning to take Kiri downtown." I falter for a moment and then agree. "We'll be there around six," Navin says before hanging up.

Inside, silence reigns. When I turn on the rig, my hands are damp, from warmth or perhaps nervousness, but slowly I lose myself in work. This room, deep in the basement, is where we electrophysiologists barricade ourselves from the dancing robots, fizz-bang experiments, and jumbo scanners of the more flamboyant researchers.

When Navin and Kiri arrive, the laboratory has emptied. I am the last one, still trying to catch up.

"Momma, we're here," my son says. "We're here."

I take him in my arms. Navin is holding Kiri's discarded hat and mittens. They bubble, ripe with colour, from his pockets.

"You're warm," Kiri says. "See how warm you are.

"We walked all the way from Côte-des-Neiges," he says proudly. "Down the big hill and then we saw a hawk but it didn't come too close." Unzipping his coat, he goes directly to the Zeiss. He looks into the microscope, studies the slide for a moment, and lapses into a contemplative silence. The first time my son came here, he was four years old. He had gazed at a neuron, lithe as a starburst, stained Nile blue. My son knows about pipettes and single-unit recording, he knows that there are neurons and also glia, that Aplysia is a kind of marine snail, and that the brain, full of currents and chemistry, is never at rest.

Navin goes from microscope to microscope, peering down, in case one of my colleagues has left a slide behind, a bit of hippocampus.

I go to him and touch his elbow. One of his arms folds over me like a wing. I tell him, "I'm glad you came."

From his pocket he takes out a small, porcelain owl. "We saw this on the way and thought of you." In my hand it feels like a polished stone, hollowed out, alive and perfect.

"Ma," Kiri calls. "Come look. Aplysia."

I go to him and put my eyes to the lens. Kiri rests his fingertips against my hip.

Bit by bit, one micromillimetre at a time, I lower the tip of a glass electrode toward the neuron. My head feels heavy, but somehow the pipette glides with stoic precision. Anaesthetized, pinned flat, cut open with surgical scissors, this innocent creature and her brethren have given me more cells than I dare count. I feel as if I can operate on Aplysia blindfolded: first, removing a tangle of nerves, then, carefully, delicately, extracting a particular neuron and its spindly axon, the axon sagging out like fishing line. Aplysia was the first creature I studied long ago, in Vancouver. In the sea, she looks like a petal swirling through the water, her gills clapping softly together.

When the electrode is touching the cellular fluid, I increase the voltage, waiting, hand on the dial of the amplifier, until the neuron fires. Here it comes: my signal amp is connected to a speaker, so we can hear the cell itself. *Boom. Boom.* It sounds like artillery fire, like a parade.

This is Kiri's favourite part. "What's he saying?" my son asks.

I close my eyes, listening. "He's saying, 'Open the door, let me in! I have a message!'"

"Come in, come in," Kiri whispers. "Tell me."

My son's lashes, long and frail, are like tiny wingtips. I kneel down, touching his shoulders. They seem frighteningly small, weightless.

"Where does a thought come from, Momma?"

"From what we see. From the world inside us."

He considers this. "Can you *make* a thought?" he asks. "Can you grow one in a dish?"

"Soon we'll grow everything in dishes," Navin says.

I smile. "Not yet."

My son looks at me searchingly. "I'm waiting for you," he says. He is trying to tell me something more, to make things right. The incomprehension in his eyes cracks my heart. I hold him and whisper in his ear. He says, "It was a mistake. Just a mistake."

Navin comes to us.

Together, we put on our hats and scarves. I lock the door of the lab and then we go into the clear night. They continue, hand in hand, toward the stores and lights on St. Catherine Street. They have the same loping gait, their bodies sway, like paper boats, from side to side. For a long time, I stand there, trying to keep sight of them. They fade into the crowd. I turn in the other direction and begin walking back.

We kept the secret, Kiri and I. When Navin came home and saw the discoloured skin on his son's face, Kiri said he had fallen at school. I let the lie stand. It had happened once. In a moment that seemed so large and inescapable, anger had suffocated me and then, just as quickly, dissolved. A few weeks later, Navin went away to London. I tried not to be alone with my son but Kiri, so small and confused, followed me from room to room. "You're not here," he kept saying. "Why aren't you here?" I went out of the house and stood in the cold, desperate to find the way through. I told myself that I could fix things, I must stop what was happening.

In the apartment I turned the heat up high, but still my hands shook. The water came to me, everywhere, loud. Something had spilled on the kitchen floor and Kiri was walking through it, running, stamping his feet. I asked him to stop. My thoughts didn't fit together. I heard noises all around us, I saw shapes coming nearer and Kiri shouting, oblivious. *Stop*, I said again. I tried to leave but he gripped my hands. I pulled away, but he was holding my clothes. I tried to free myself. In a moment of wildness, he grabbed a handful of forks and threw them down into the mess. The noise seemed like the ceiling crashing down, falling on top of us, blocking all the light. I raised my hand and hit him, once, twice. I cannot remember it all. And then, in an instant, the noise disappeared.

He was sitting on the floor, gasping, "I'm sorry, I'm sorry."

I knelt beside him, in shock. When I looked into his face, the bruise terrified me, I saw my child curled up, I smelled a burning in the room. He saw me watching him. "Don't be scared," Kiri said. "I'm going to fix everything. You don't have to be scared of me."

When we lay down that night, he asked me to stop crying, he said I had been crying for days. "What's happening to you?"

"I don't know, Kiri."

He gazed at me, his eyes older now, beginning to understand. "You have to know," he said softly. "You have to."

Night after night, in the days that followed, he came into my room. "You're dreaming," he said, waking me. "Stop dreaming. Please stop dreaming." He would crawl into the bed, saying that he was cold, that he did not want to sleep alone. I was afraid to hold my son. One day, Kiri called his father without my knowing. Bravely, he told Navin to return home, that I was ill. He didn't know how else to describe what we were going through.

Frantic, Navin took the first flight back. I told him everything. At first, he didn't believe, couldn't believe.

"Ask him," I told him. "Please."

It was January, and the ice covered everything and I didn't know anymore, I couldn't explain, how this could have happened, why I could not control my hands, my own body. We went through the motions, going to school, going to work, but something inside me, inside Navin, was dying. The broken world finally fell apart. Our son didn't understand and I saw that he blamed himself, that he tried so hard not to be the cause of my rage, my unpredictable anger. He aspired to a sort of perfection, as if it were up to him to keep us safe. We sat down with Kiri. I told my son that the only person to blame was myself. I told him that I had to go away for a little while.

"No," he said to his father. "Please don't do this. I take everything back."

Navin came to Hiroji's apartment carrying a box of my books, Lena's picture, and a photograph he had taken of Kiri and me at the fairgrounds, La Ronde, the bright halo of the Ferris wheel behind us, neon colours stretching across our skin. He set the box down, weeping without seeming to realize there were tears. He asked me why I had never confided in him, how we had let it come to this. He had been my lover for more than a decade and yet, he said, I remained a stranger to him. Navin wandered around Hiroji's apartment, taking in the dusty shelves, the pillow and blanket on the couch.

"I know you," he said. "I've always known you."

I struggled to understand. I remembered a whiteness that came, debilitating, that I tried to remove from my body. One morning, Navin brought me a letter from Meng, who planned to travel back to Cambodia and wanted me to go with him. There were things, he said, that we needed to talk about, to end. Night after night I tried to bring back the ones I had left behind. In the mornings, when I opened my eyes, I saw only the bare walls. Everything, the good and the selfish, the loved and the feared, had taken refuge inside me. Thirty years later and still I remembered everything.

The telephone wakes me. The cat startles, tips sideways, and runs away. Her paws drum along the hardwood floors as I wave my hand into the darkness, closing my fingers around the receiver. Navin. Before I can say hello, the person on the other end, a woman's voice, has begun speaking.

"Tavy," I say, interrupting her, fighting my way out from under a net of sleep. Bit by bit, the room sharpens. I struggle for Khmer words. "What time is it there?"

A long pause and I'm suspended on the line. "I'm not sure. I'm at the office, at DC-Cam. Maybe four in the afternoon?"

Four in the morning, then, in Montreal.

"But, you see," she says, "I'm returning your call. You left a message last night."

I start to say it wasn't urgent but Tavy continues, cutting me off firmly. "I found something. There are letters, beginning in 1975. We found six, all addressed to James Matsui."

I fumble for the lights and end up knocking over a glass of water. "Tavy, wait. Letters from whom? From someone in Canada?"

"No," she says. She slows down, realizing now that I was sound asleep. "A young woman. Cambodian. All this time, since 1996, these letters were in the archives. They were filed under her name. *Sorya*. But now we're updating the database, right? Everything is going into the computer. More key words, anything to help us identify people. After I got your message, I re-did the search for James Matsui, but I found Sorya's file instead. He had donated the letters.

"Listen," she says. I hear movement, papers sorted through. Tavy begins to read, "*My darling James, today is the first day of the New Year. Heng came today and returned your camera . . .*" She keeps going.

The water spreads in a puddle, touching my bare feet.

"She was his wife," Tavy says. "Maybe Sorya is not her only name, probably she had an alias, many aliases. Nearly everyone did. I should look . . ."

"James wasn't married. Or Hiroji never mentioned it."

"But according to what she wrote . . ." Voices in the background, rising and falling. "She thought her letters were being smuggled to James," Tavy says. Her voice is low, it mirrors my own surprise. "She took a risk and gave these letters to someone she trusted. Whoever it was, they told her that James Matsui was in hiding in the northeast, in the caves by the Cambodia–Laos border. Who knows if it was true? But in late 1975, she was arrested. I found her prison dossier – the usual, her biography, confessions, and also her photograph. There is nothing after 1976. But, also, there is no date of death.

"I'll keep looking," she says after a moment. "The letters are scanned so I can send them by email. I'm sorry I woke you . . . Usually when we find this kind of information, people like to know right away. One last thing, when James Matsui donated the letters, he left a phone number. I tried calling it but the number is out of service."

"Thank you, Tavy," I say.

"Yes," she says. "I'll keep looking."

The dial tone hums in my ear. I hang up, step across the puddle of water, kneel down, and begin to wipe it with a T-shirt. The starlight is dim, a fine wash against the window. The water seems to keep on spreading. I give up on the puddle. On it goes, touching the feet of the couch, swelling against the carpet.

Unable to sleep, I go to Hiroji's office and open the file.

Wednesday, February 22
[fragment]

This is the way Hiroji once described it to me. In 1976, Nuong arrived, alone, at the Aranyaprathet camp in Thailand. He had been ten years old when he and his brothers escaped from their cooperative, a mountain camp outside of Sisophon. The six boys had walked into the jungle and they had survived, on roots and stolen watermelons, for more than a month, finding their way west, toward Thailand. They scaled the Dangrek Mountains and descended into a dry, open forest. But then the mines separating Cambodia from Thailand, mines planted by the Khmer Rouge, began. The detonators were the size of melon seeds and the colour of rust, with trip wires, luminous nylon thread, that curled through the grass. The brothers walked single file, the eldest first, and Nuong last. Nuong saw only the black shirts of his brothers ahead of him. They whispered to him not to panic, not to be afraid. But leaving Cambodia was like trying to walk through a forest of glass. They set off a series of mines. Within seconds, all of his brothers were dead.

For a long time, he stood where he was. Bits of earth were everywhere around him, they fell in clumps from the trees, triggering yet more explosions. A deer leapt toward him, the ground burst. He stood with his hands pressed to his ears believing that he, too, had come apart. He saw his brothers again. They were impatient and they yelled at him to hurry, so Nuong closed his eyes and did as he was told. He began to crawl. Flies covered him. He was less than twenty metres from the border, he crossed without knowing it, and kept going until a Thai farmer saw him, reached down, and carried him away.

In 1980, Nuong was sponsored by a family in Lowell, Massachusetts, and he lifted off for America. For nearly two years, his letters arrived at Hiroji's apartment every month, the upright alphabet giving way to cursive, to scribbled notes, and then to postcards. By the time Nuong was a teenager, even those no longer came. The boy had passed through a curtain, he belonged to a new family.

And then, last summer, Hiroji had answered the telephone and a voice he didn't recognize, with an unfamiliar accent, said, "It's me, Nick."

"Nick?" Hiroji said. "I'm sorry. Who is this?"

"Nuong," the voice said after a moment. "Nuong. From Aran camp."

Hiroji was overjoyed. He asked a handful of questions but Nuong managed to evade them all. After a few minutes of dodging and deflecting, he told Hiroji that he was in trouble.

"What's happened? Let me help you."

But by then it was too late to intervene. Nuong had made too many mistakes, starting with the wrong friends, a quick temper, drinking, drugs, and finally a vicious fight that ended up blinding a man. Nuong and his adoptive family had not realized that, despite Nuong's papers – his refugee status in the United States, his high school diploma, his green card – he was not an American citizen. He had neglected to apply. Instead, he was a refugee who had committed a felony and, now, under the law, he was subject to deportation. He was being sent back, forcibly, to Phnom Penh.

"We'll get a lawyer," Hiroji said.

"But I have one already."

"I have a friend in Boston, don't worry about money –"

"No," Nuong said. "I just wanted to tell you. I wanted you to know that I was going back. That it was all for nothing."

Hiroji was stunned silent.

"I don't even speak Khmer anymore, I barely remember the language," Nuong said. He laughed hurriedly, and then the discomfort came back. Hiroji saw the sullen Thai soldiers and the Khmer Rouge who had come like spiders across the border, taking truckloads of refugees. He saw the small boy who would sleep at the foot of his bed, motionless, unblinking.

"Nuong," Hiroji began.

"I don't even know if that's my name. It's what my brothers called me. It's just the name I remember."

In November, a few weeks before Hiroji disappeared, he had received a letter from Nuong. Hiroji told me that the boy's American family had gone to visit him in Phnom Penh. They had decided to invest in a small hotel that Nuong was now managing. *The Lowell Hotel*, Nuong wrote. *Their idea*. Here was his telephone number, here was his address. *Send me a photograph of James*, Nuong wrote. *Don't forget. I want to keep looking.*

Hiroji told me that he remembered following Nuong to the border. The boy stood there, in the dry, sunlit field, holding a stone in his hands, staring across the bridge. The Khmer Rouge guard taunted Nuong to step forward, to throw the stone, to cross the bridge back into Cambodia, to come home, but the boy just stood there staring like a sick dog, a dying child. Come home. If you come home, Angkar will give you everything you want. "Nuong," Hiroji had called. But he already knew what would happen. This was a country, he had learned, in which no one responded to their names. Names were empty syllables, signifying nothing, lost as easily as a suit of clothes, a brother or a sister, an entire world.

[end]

Unable to settle, I put the espresso maker on the stove. While the coffee warbles up through its pipes, I free a chocolate bar from its wrapper, set it near the element so that it melts a little in the heat, and then I carry it to Hiroji's desk, eating it slowly.

Tavy's email has arrived, along with the scans of Sorya's file. *My darling James*, Sorya's letters begin. There are six of them, dating from April 1975 to the end of that year.

I read them through once, and then again. The screen glows whitely in the dark room and outside all is hushed. From the pocket of my coat, I retrieve the yellow notebook and open it to the back cover where Nuong's number is written. The cat comes in and begins to clean herself as I dial. The line rings several times and then a man answers.

In English, I ask for Ly Nuong.

"Yes. Speaking. Who is this?"

I tell him my name and say that I am a friend of Hiroji Matsui. That I am looking for him. Brusquely, the man says that I have the wrong number, that I am mis-informed. In Khmer, I ask Nuong not to hang up, I have found something that might lead to Hiroji's brother, James. I tell him about the letters, written by Sorya, about Tavy at the Documentation Centre, and the file Hiroji gave me last year. I ask for his help and then, abruptly, the words stop. I say my name again.

"He's already gone."

The words don't register.

Nuong says. "Hiroji is in Laos."

I ask him a string of questions. *When, how, where.*

"Wait," Nuong says. "Slow down. I won't hang up. I'm listening."

We talk for a long time. Near the end of our conversation he tells me that, when he first arrived in America, at the age of eleven, it wasn't the war he had left behind – the refugee camps, the Khmer Rouge – that had struck him as incomprehensible. Rather, he was confounded by the vastness of this new country. America's bright smiles and proud efficiency, its endlessly flowing water, cinemas, fairgrounds, and easy optimism, shamed him. He felt out of place, unknowable.

"Here in Phnom Penh, in Sisophon," Nuong says, "people went on. The *mulatan* are still there. Some are farmers, some are soldiers. Nobody had anyplace to go. And all the new people, the April 17 people who couldn't leave, they've gone back to the cities where they began." He says that hardly anyone outside the country remembers this war. Only us, only here.

I tell Nuong that I don't think I can ever return.

He understands. "Hiroji is in Laos," he says. "I can tell you where he's staying."

That night, I dream of Navin. I dream and when I wake, the curtains are open, the blanket is twisted around me, and the air smells of rumdul flowers and smoke and the river. I get up and go to the door and open it but no one is there, no cars, only the faint glow of the streetlamps. I stand for a moment and let the cold sharpen my senses, invade my dreams. When I first arrived in Montreal, this city had seemed so alien to me, so self-contained and mysterious. How many winters have I passed here? Nearly a decade's worth, the cold months accumulating, white and silent, the years opening toward another existence. I remember the warmth of Navin's apartment when I first met him. We were like two coins left in the bottom of the jar: here by circumstance and luck, here together. It was dawn the first time we made our way to the bedroom, dawn when the building began to wake, when his neighbours prepared breakfast, gathered their children, packed their bags and briefcases, jingled their keys. I smelled coffee through the walls but I was holding Navin. Doors slamming upstairs, downstairs, and Navin watching as I touched my lips to him, as I knelt on the blanket. His lean body, surprisingly strong, dark in the unlit room. The building emptying, the air disappearing. I pushed the windows open, back then I craved the shock of air on my skin. In the beginning, we never talked about Cambodia or Malaysia. Our countries remained behind us, two lamps dimming. Like his father, who died young, Navin was an engineer. When I met him, he had just come back from Kuala Lumpur and its towering, silvery skyscrapers. He took me to hear ice melting on the St. Lawrence River, a steady crackling and firing. In the kitchen, there was a picture of his father. They had the same narrow face and dark eyes, the same solemn beauty. I had no photographs from my childhood. "Describe your father to me," Navin had said. He was making lunch for us, a thin, savoury roti canai. His cooking filled with air with heat, with a floury residue.

"Tell me what he was like."

I told Navin how easy it had been to make my father laugh, how his hands had danced when he spoke, clipping and prodding the air. I remembered how my father's entire body had always seemed to lean forwards, propelled into the future, how my brother and I had to run just to keep up with him. I remember how, at weddings and celebrations, he was always the first to start dancing the *ramvong*, how he never slept well, how he stood on the balcony singing to himself. "What songs?" Navin asked. I remembered. My father had told me they were the songs of my grandmother.

On the residential streets outside Navin's apartment, brick duplexes had stood, shoulder to shoulder, exhaling chimney smoke, all along the boulevard. Growing up, I remember arak singers trying to tempt wandering souls, the *pralung*, back into their bodies. I remember celebrations, ceremonies, the words Meng had spoken before I flew away to Canada. Your daughter is crossing the ocean. You, too, must go on. You, too, must walk to your own destiny.

⁘

In the sky on the way to Saigon, the hours pass slowly. The plane sails on, food arrives and disappears, trays fold up, windows darken. The man seated beside me watches one movie after another, he laughs big belly laughs and then falls asleep, his headphones askew, his blanket slipping across his shoulders.

I had gone to see my family last night. Navin told me Kiri had started a new set of drawings. Aplysia, waving like a flower. One cell, two cells, or Aplysia its entirety, a wide creature billowing through the ocean. At the kitchen table, Kiri sat across from me and asked me where I was going. "To Laos," I said. "To see Hiroji." Morrin had given me two weeks of leave. In my son's bedroom, I put my fingers to the globe, turned the Earth on its pedestal, and showed him the place. The names inscribed were in French. *Cambodge*, he read. *Viêt Nam. Laos.*

Kiri gave me a drawing to bring with me.

I touched the blue, waxy openness. "The sky," I said. "Or maybe the ocean?"

He nodded. "It goes off the edge of the page." At school, he said, they had been looking at images from the Hubble telescope. "See? Like a galaxy, and you can go forever but the universe, it just never ends."

He looked at Taka the Old, who would be staying with them while I was away. When they left for Vancouver, Navin's sister would come to house-sit. "This cat has a big nose," he said, suddenly interested. "Like a rabbit."

"You're part of us," Navin told me when I left. "We're your family. We have to find a way."

Now, the flight attendant hands out ice cream that we eat with spoons shaped like tiny wooden paddles. I pace up and down in the aisles, between one set of dark blue curtains and another. Nearly everyone is sleeping, heads turned to the side. Hours later, as we are lowering toward Vietnam, I can see the Mekong River, I see temples like patches of gold, the delicate crowns of trees, dry fields ready for the next season. I breathe it in, this landscape so like Cambodia's, like a painting I memorized long ago, shade by shade, curve after curve. Gamboge, the colour, was named by Flemish painters some three hundred years ago, after my country, Kampuchea. Cambodia. Deep yellow, burned orange, saffron, the colour of the monk's robes, of tigers and the petalled eaves of the Khmer temples. I can't stop looking. I am trying to follow this path to its end, I am trying to continue by buying a ticket, pushing my bag through the X-ray scanner, folding myself into the impossible drawer of seat 23D, flying away from Montreal, through the rough turbulence that joins these continents. In Saigon, when we exited the airplane, heat came suddenly, thick and heavy. In the airport, I drank tea. I bought post-cards of the south coast. Women in *ao dai* and women in slacks, men my father's age, businessmen in polyester suits, the ones who had survived the long wars and now crossed and recrossed the sky, hurried past me. A judder-ing, unhappy plane carried me north to Vientiane, Laos, and from there I took a bus twelve hours over the moun-tains. A wet humidity enveloped us. I could not under-stand the language. Some Lao words drew images in my thoughts but most were puzzles to me. This country was so mesmerizing, the bus climbed up into the moun-tains, slowing in the high altitudes, descending through limestone valleys and supine clouds. There was a woman on the road with her worried chickens. Little children torpedoed baguette sandwiches through the windows of the bus in return for a few thousand kip. I imagined Kiri here. Where are you going? a woman asked me. I don't know, I said. She smiled and smiled. I cried and no one noticed. I wanted to go home but this was as close as I could bring myself, floating by sea, floating in air.

The bus carried me to the ancient city of Luang Prabang, where I stayed for two nights, waiting, think-ing. In my bare hotel room, I spoke to Navin. We talked about our son. Navin told me about the years in Malaysia, after his father had passed away, and he and his sister were left to raise themselves. He told me details that we had never shared before, afraid of pity or misunderstanding, unwilling to give meaning to the past. I fell asleep thinking of telescopes, microscopes. Galileo and his polished mirrors, how they carried, magically, more visible light to the eye, making the tiny things large, and the distant stars near. How they collapsed space and time. The next morning, I arranged a ride to the village that Nuong had described to me, a dirt road with fifteen or twenty wooden houses and two small restaurants. By then it was late February, almost three months since Hiroji had disappeared. I was let off beside the village temple and the truck driver, a boy in his late teens, smiled at me wistfully. It was Monday, late afternoon. When the truck heaved away, the rising dust hung before me. A tired light veiled the temple, which was painted red and gold, lush as a woman's fancy dress, like a tirade against the brown landscape. I waited. This village was so small, news would spread within a few minutes that a stranger was here. I stood beneath a blossoming tree and children came out of nowhere to peek at me, and I wondered if I had been like this, Sopham and I, fascinated by the strangers on the riverfront, with all our lives ahead of us. My mother once told me that we are born, into the world, whole. Year by year, our heads grow crowded with too many voices, too many lives. We begin to splinter apart. We take in too much, too many people and places, we try to keep them inside us where the world won't alter them.

This is what I saw then: a Japanese man wearing a light blue, pinstriped shirt, creased as if it has just come from the store, and dark slacks. He wore no hat, carried no cane, had neither glasses nor sunglasses. His loafers were scuffed. He was clean-shaven, thin in a ragged way, he walked well but slowly, his face was sun-darkened and deeply lined.

He came toward me, the same as I remembered but softer, older. Another man stood behind him, so alike in appearance, so different in bearing. It must be a trick of light, I thought, we are separating and merging, intersecting and dividing.

"Janie," Hiroji said. "Is that you?"

My friend held me for a long time.

"Don't cry," he said. "You're here."

❖

In James's house, the walls and floors were built of wood and bamboo, the structure stood on wooden stilts, and evening light ran in as if through a straw basket. Hiroji's brother had been living here for almost a decade. James was very quiet. He moved in the corners, he set a table for us but when it came time to eat, he went away into another room and shut the door behind him. Hiroji served sticky rice that came from a conical basket, and some kind of wild green whose name I didn't know, and a clear, rich soup. He asked me about Montreal, and I told

him about the winter, about Kiri and Navin, the things
that had happened. I kept glancing into his face, trying
to reassure myself that he was here. Hiroji was quiet and
for long moments he stared awkwardly at his hands. He
told me that he had been with James for a month, that
when he found his brother, James had not recognized
him. Hiroji had wanted to go home to Montreal but
he didn't know how and, at night, lying in bed, he was
overcome by shame. "I couldn't explain this," he said,
gesturing to the room, the closed door, the village, "and
so I put off writing to you. I didn't know how to begin."
In Laos, he said, one could abandon the past and become
someone else. But to what end? He was lost here. His
brother did not seem to need or want him.

Hiroji took off his glasses and folded the arms down.

"Is it really James?" I asked.

He nodded, meeting my eyes. "But now I'm here,
and he's here, and . . . there's no way for me to cross the
last few steps." He smiled, embarrassed. "I had pictured
things so differently."

The village had fallen still. We finished our drinks
and then Hiroji showed me the rooms upstairs. He offered me his but I wanted to sleep on the open veranda,
surrounded by the humid air. He acquiesced.

"Good night, Janie," he said, and then he left me.

Under the mosquito net, I heard the jungle that ran
along behind the village and climbed up the mountains.
It was the first time in many years that I'd heard those

sounds and when I finally fell asleep, I felt protected because the jungle never ceased, there was no such thing as silence or purity, there was no such thing as an ending even though all my life I'd been looking and keeping faith.

In the morning, a thunderstorm came, threads of lightning connecting the earth to the clouds. When Hiroji went into town for supplies, James and I sat outside in the diffuse, changing light. A woman brought us coffee and sat with us. She was Khmer and we began speaking, in tangents and in drifting conversations, and eventually James, too, began to speak. The days and nights we remembered began to overlap. Afterwards, and in the days that followed, I wrote so many things. I did not know what I was making. Terrible dreams came, but I tried to let them run through me and reach the ground. I saw that they would always return, this was the shape of my life, this was where the contours lay, this was the form. Yet I wanted, finally, to be the one to describe it. To decide on the dreams that took root in me.

As I work, my son comes to me in my memory. Kiri names the rivers for me just as I once taught him: *St. Lawrence, Fraser, Kootenay, Mackenzie, Yukon, Chaudière, Assiniboine.* Words to keep him company, to name the world, to contain it.

James

❖

Monday, February 27
[fragment]

The hills are a fading purple, already the colour of dusk.
James Matsui knows these mountains well, they are visible from Phnom Penh, the capital of Cambodia, a once-
elegant city that now sleeps with one eye open, like Cain
dreaming of Abel. In October 1974, on a night when trails
of mortar fire glint in the southern skies, James writes
the last letter that he will send to his family in Canada.
He takes the envelope to the Red Cross office and then he
detours beside the river, the Tonle Sap. He is lost in the
crowd. Couples brush past him holding hands, children
strut along the boulevard, tall as peacocks, parading past
the throng of beggars. They and he are surreal in the
evening light, dissolving in and out of focus, strolling to
the rhythmic boom of artillery fire. Around him, people
giggle in response to the shelling, maybe to prove they
aren't afraid, or maybe because the long war has made
everyone careless or shameless or easily amused. On the
boulevard, young swindlers in military uniforms stop

the traffic. He doesn't like the look of them, not when the stinking, starving man letting them pass is their grandfather's age, not when beggar boys swarm at their feet waiting for treasure. He can't abide their rifles and their ammunition belts, their cheap, flagrant uniforms. This is a city about to fall.

That night he works the midnight shift at the refugee camp and in the morning, his driver delivers him home to bed. Sorya is there, in her slippers, twisting the radio dial back and forth, catching mostly static.

They married a year ago. Sorya's brother, Dararith, had been a Red Cross doctor, a Cambodian doctor (James is in the habit of differentiating, and he finds it hard to break this habit). Sometimes the three of them would stay up late talking about the war, about movies and TV shows and rock music. Dararith was an average doctor but a brilliant singer. He used to serenade them on those long nights when they bunkered down to wait out the shelling. James and Sorya get by in Khmer and crusts of French and English. She is well read and polite and funny, but sometimes, lately, for split seconds, he knows that she wants to hit him, or fling something heavy at him. For his carelessness, the way the war no longer touches him. Sometimes he comes to bed and wonders why she's there, what she wants from him, why she keeps her eyes closed when they have sex, why she makes him come so hard and almost bitterly, and then she rolls out from under him and leaves the room so that he falls asleep to

his own solitary breathing. It's this ridiculous war that
drags on and on and gradually covers everyone in dust
so that, in the end, it would be just a small step to crumble
like the stone buildings and the once-paved roads, to
accept the degradation.

The Red Cross had sent him to Saigon in 1971 but he
couldn't abide the depressed, strung-out Americans. His
superiors said, Well, try Cambodia, so up the river he
went, a boy on a barge looking for better company. And
it was better for a while, especially when Dararith was
here. Phnom Penh wasn't as frenetic, it wasn't so obvi-
ously a lost cause. But what was once intoxicating to him
is now dreary, Phnom Penh is catching up to Saigon. The
end is near and everyone who doesn't know it is either a
diplomat or a king. The barbarians are at the gates with
their rubber sandals and their Chinese-made rockets
and it's useless now, worrying over the bombing runs,
legal or illegal, even though he sees the damage every
day, thousands crawling into the city with missing limbs
and missing children, people mutilated by the Khmer
Rouge or bombed into hysteria by the Americans. They
appear like wraiths. He knows men who have thrown
themselves into the Tonle Bati, even Dararith used to
joke about it. Nothing changes, he used to say. We're
caught in an infinite war.

But he, James, is living off the fat of the land: a noble
Red Cross doctor healing children who will be pushed
to the front lines tomorrow, boys who, day by day, are

learning to revel in their worst tendencies. Tomorrow, he could be in Bangkok. Today there was an old woman eating the bark off a tree, stripping ribbons from it the way his mother used to de-vein the celery stalks, and he didn't have the energy to go home and fetch this old woman some sugar and chocolate, something from his magnificent store of abandoned goods, bequeathed to him by the fickle bureaucrats, expatriates, and socialites leaving Phnom Penh en masse. What would his mother say? She saw the war in Tokyo. She saw much worse than this. The black dust covers everyone, even the healers. *Physician, heal thy self*, but what he wants is to sleep for days on end and wake up in a tropical paradise where a compassionate Buddha smiles down on him and touches his golden fingertips to the dirt to remind James of what we are and what we must be, dust to dust, being to nothingness, and how we err in the pursuit of an existence more lasting.

"You never understood God," his mother used to say.

He had teased her by answering, "Why is it that God always fails to understand me?"

The hours are passing. The smell of fried food wafts thickly in through the porous walls. Morning light shifts across the bed, across the walls, into his open hand. It's so distressingly beautiful here, so deformed and alive.

———

Sorya tries to make the bed with him still in it. This, he knows, is her quiet way of telling him that it's past noon and a man should not be so slovenly. He doesn't like speaking Khmer in the morning, before breakfast, so he addresses her in English. Let me sleep a little longer. She brings him a cup of coffee and he feels like a wet-nosed boy home sick from school. Her fingertips smell of anise. He drinks, burns his tongue, and then he pulls her back into bed with him, strips her, fucks her, tells her to forget everything but him. He says this in English and she answers in Khmer. In the end they speak the same loop-holed language that says only a little and lets the big things slide through.

"James," she had said when they first met. "What a serious name."

She is clever and fearless, she married him for practical reasons, and she will never be completely grateful. She once said that war makes people say far too many things, good and bad, that they'll regret in calmer times.

"But are peaceful days around the corner?" James had asked, wanting to provoke her.

"Sure," she said. "Wars always end. Peace always ends. People get tired."

Sorya doesn't stay in bed past six a.m. What she does, he can't imagine. The schools are closed and have been for months, so she has no job to report to.

He remembers the days they went to the disco-theque, Dararith bought the beer but they gambled with James's cash. Dararith steered the moped that ferried them around but usually James and Sorya had to walk home without him, picking their way through the rubble. Dararith, he pursued women as if they were keys on a ring, and he was always falling in love because his brand of affection was endearingly sudden. Sorya was glamorous with her black hair loose and her bare shoulders and calf-high boots, her market-stall clothing that she wore like high fashion. She carried herself like a girl who'd been to Paris, to New York, but it was all show. Television, she told him, on one of those awkward walks home, can be a gifted teacher. And books. She married James, maybe, for his books. Something to distract her while she waited for her brother to come back, but it's been two years and it's obvious by now that people don't come back.

She doesn't wear makeup anymore but her hair is still long. Unbrushed, it floods around her and it seems, to James, as if it eats the light and hides the things that no one says: I married you as a favour to Dararith, I married you because of the war, out of loneliness, out of fear. I love only you. They both think these things, they both hold themselves in reserve.

"James," she says now. "It's a good name but it doesn't suit you."

"King James."

She pushes the covers aside, stands up. When did she get so thin, so melancholy?

"Don't leave me," he tells her but then he is suddenly embarrassed.

"I hate sleeping alone," he explains and she turns, a half-smile on her face, a half-sadness.

The war was ending and he worked all the time. The storehouses were empty, he had no medicine, no needles, saline, or chloroquine, no bandages, no aspirin or dysentery pills. He patted shoulders, amputated limbs, blinked into the persistent heat, and turned his back on the worst cases. It was the cool season, supposedly, but his clothes were sweat-drenched by ten in the morning. In his gut was a feeling of panic mixed with the weight of inertia, he was light-headed and joyous and bitterly angry. The radio spewed bulletins from the war in Vietnam and the shaming of the Americans not only there but here in Cambodia and next door in Laos. Ask the diplomats – American, French, English – and this humiliation was everyone's fault but their own. Ask the Cambodians what would happen next and they just shrugged and smiled their fatalistic smiles. James hoped it was the last time he would live in a place where no one carried any responsibility, where the days were predetermined by the hundred lives already lived, by a thousand acts of karma, by destiny that rubbed out other destinations. He was sick of this country and he would have left already if it weren't for Sorya, that's what he tells himself. But every day he goes back to the camps and the Red Cross shelters and feels strangely at peace. Ten years ago, he was smoking pot in a dive on Powell Street, coming home blinkered, but his mother and Hiroji, true innocents, never noticed a thing. When he gets high it reminds him of how the air burned his throat in Tokyo when he was small, how he was terrified of fire, and then the long journey by boat and plane and bus that took them to Vancouver where everything was green, where things were young and not skeletal, but still he was so fucking scared. Japan was finished, his father said, even the ground was poisoned but now, *Now we go from fire to water, from the city to the sea.* He had turned the words into a song, a nursery rhyme. His father had been a professor of medicine at Tokyo University, he had been a solemn, determined man, but the supreme effort of getting them out of postwar Japan had ruined his health. When his contacts in America disappointed him, he had turned to England. In the end, he settled for Canada. A year after they reached Vancouver, his father died, post-stroke, on a crisp, white bed in a Canadian hospital. James remembered the place well, the sharp, stingy smell of it and the squawk of rubber soles on the icy floors. Be brave, his father had told him, and all the while his kid brother had pressed his pink face against his mother's skin and slept in ignorant bliss.

His mother had opened a dry goods shop on Powell

Street and James had taken his first paper route, his first of many: *The Vancouver Sun*, the *Province*, the *Sing Tao Daily*. Hiroji used to lie on the mat in the back of the store and coo at them, and the baby's cooing made James feel improbably wise. He was eleven years old when he told his baby brother that they would both be doctors, real professionals. Maybe Tokyo and his father had given him a taste for calamity, maybe he had inherited his father's uneasy, chafing mind. He scraped through medical school, finished his residency. The Vietnam War was in full swing and he signed up with the Red Cross. When all hell broke loose, he preferred to be busy and not just standing around. Saigon was fine, but Cambodia is something else, manic depressive, split with contradictions. They take him for local here, a regular Chinese-Khmer slogging through the mud.

On the night he travelled from Phnom Penh to Neak Luong, he packed and unpacked three times, removing his camera, adding his journal. Removing bandages and adding chocolate and whiskey. Overhead, helicopters circled and he told Sorya, "Maybe it's better if you come with me."

"I don't think so," she said.

He was on his way east and he realized she was right. Any day now, Neak Luong would fall to the Khmer Rouge. Probably he'd be shot by a sniper, or his boat would be shelled, or some hideous Communist maquis would poach him and serve him for supper.

"Write me a letter," she said and they smiled because the postal system was a joke.

"Take this money," James said, "and buy us two tickets for Bangkok."

"Honestly, you want to leave Phnom Penh? This heaven."

"Do you?"

She laughed. "All this time, I only stayed because of you."

"Don't joke," he said, confused.

"Careful in the wild," she said. "Don't come home dressed in black, carrying an AK, and wearing rubber sandals. I'll shoot you on sight."

"I'll come in a stampede of elephants."

Her eyes teased him with restrained laughter. The foolish things he would do, the foolish dances he would perform, to make her laugh.

"In better days," he said, "we'll go to the sea."

"Promise me."

He saw the lines at the corners of her eyes, he heard something in her voice, a foreboding, a hopelessness he'd tried so hard to banish with bravado, with laughter. What other avenue was left them? Every day they were surrounded by corpses, women without faces, men without limbs.

"Yes," he said. "I do promise."

—

They were ambushed in the dark. The cruddy boat tipped right then left, and James had a crushing sense of déjà vu as black-clothed creatures lifted from the water and slithered into the boat. He wondered whether Sorya would open the cache of money he had left her, whether any tickets remained for Bangkok, whether she would stay or go. For a split second, before the first kick, he thought he was being sent to join Dararith in the afterlife to which all doctors disappeared: a haven of arrogant, self-pitying men, a fate worse than hell. But this wasn't a joke. These creatures had no sense of irony. They beat him and he, a soft Canadian, was already begging for mercy after the first punch. So this is what blood tastes like, he thought. So this is what real suffering is. They threw him into a hold. He thought of his father, who'd had the good sense to pass away in a clean bed rather than down in the reeking underground, in the terrifying Tokyo shelters, and now he, King James, would pass away in the dark, sucked into the careless water. One day he would wash up, bloated and unrecognizable, onto the shore of a shitty country. He heard them shoot the boat driver. He cried harder as they threw the body away.

They kept him blindfolded all of the time. Once, when they took the blindfold off, they asked him to identify tablets they had found in his bags. The samples were pink, like cotton candy at the Pacific National Exhibition fair grounds, like orchids, a pink that seemed foolish and innocent in this burned, exhausted landscape. "These are vitamins," he said. He answered them in Khmer and they said he was a spy and he said, "No, I am not." "Where are you from?" "Japan. Tokyo." "Where is your passport?" "Lost." "Why are you here?" "To treat the wounded." "The wounded?" they said, taunting him. "You mean the Lon Nols, the traitors?" He shook his head vehemently. "I treat the people hurt by American bombs."

They covered his eyes and returned him to darkness.

With the blindfold on, he felt absurdly safe. They surrounded him: bare feet on the thirsty ground, rifles smartly reloaded, the smell of a campfire. He heard someone getting a haircut, the scissors stuttering like a solitary cricket. He heard a fire starting and water boiling, he ate mushy gruel with his hands, he itched all over from the ants in the dirt, his tongue felt cracked. Night and day, his feet were shackled, he had to piss into a foul bamboo container, he was constipated and everything hurt. He couldn't believe it was possible to be scared so long, to have his heart solidify in mute fear, and yet to continue day after day.

Sometimes, in his fantasies, he sits at his father's bedside. The blinds let in whiskers of light and he can see his father's right hand curled on the sheet, the skin over the knuckles flaccid and pale. He finds the doctors loud and the nurses kind and nobody really looks at him, not even his parents. James tells himself it's not possible to disappoint the dead. All that matters to the living is the living, that's what he had tried to explain to Sorya after her brother disappeared: "This is war, not a game. If you have the chance to escape you have to take it. If I go missing, don't sit around like a fool." He had felt like a hero when he said this.

But why waste words? Grieving Dararith, she had barely seemed to notice him. She just sat in the apartment thinking and reading, cleaning, cooking, disappearing. She didn't need his devotion and this independence, her strength, made him feel confused him and shiftless, it made him feel temporary, like an insect clinging to a drain.

Suddenly there were no more planes in the sky and no more shelling. They stopped moving around so frequently. The blindfold was removed and he found himself in a small, square storeroom, or it would have been a storeroom had there been anything on the shelves. It was comfortable enough. The floor had French cement tiles, dirty now, but the design had been lovely once. A short, efficient man came in to give him water, rice soup, and, unexpectedly, a piece of soap. Eventually, the man started to extend his visits. He sat down on the floor and asked James questions about Phnom Penh, the Red Cross, about the war in Vietnam, about food and music and religion, about his wife, about Dararith. They always spoke in Khmer. James would sit with his arms tied behind his back while the man probed him, as if his life story were a confession, as if the two were the same thing.

The man was reedy, dark-skinned, with a way of tapping his knee rhythmically with his fingertips when he spoke. He studied the ground with such intensity that James found himself looking, too, at the tiled floor, taking in the stranger's soft hands, and then the Kalashnikov laid confidently between them, the barrel of the gun covered by the cadre's Chinese cap, as if in a decorative flourish.

One morning, the man surprised James. He said, "Let me tell you about someone I once knew. A friend. I was studying at the Lycée Sisowath in Phnom Penh. Do you know it?"

"Everyone knows it."

The man went on, "This was more than twenty years ago. I lived with another boy, a Chinese-Khmer from Svay Rieng province. Are you familiar with that area?"

"Of course."

"You've been there?"

James nodded.

The man was impressed. "His mother had a petrol stand," he said, continuing. "The father was dead. The boy, Kwan, drove a lorry and he would give me lifts around the city. He was raising money for his tuition and he worked all the time."

The man's face was passive and kind, and it reminded James, disconcertingly, of his mother. His mother, too, had many surfaces, but he'd learned to see between the blinds, behind the clean edges.

"Kwan was trustworthy," the man said. His voice dropped, not quite a whisper. "Can I tell you that I trusted him more than the friends I went to school with? Those were lazy boys who never worked. Inside their empty heads they didn't even understand the concept of work. I started to tutor him. He got up very early to drive the lorry but, in the afternoons, when everyone slept, I gave him lessons. He was quick. The thing about Kwan was, he was mute. He could read lips, he could adapt, but he never, ever spoke. I confess, I was fascinated by Kwan. Boys my age were malleable. We swallowed each and every lesson without chewing it first. But Kwan, he was apart. He kept his thoughts to himself and he kept his peace.

"When you first arrived, I was astonished. I said to myself, Maybe Kwan got an education after all! Maybe he paid his way to medical school and made himself a gentleman. I congratulated myself that I, alone, had recognized you."

In the room, a mosquito buzzed at James's cheek and he wondered how the insect had found its way into the locked room where there were no windows and the air was stale. It must have come in with the man.

"Are you Kwan?"

"No."

Generously, the man extended his hand and hushed the mosquito away. "Can you be certain?"

James didn't know what to say. Now there were insects thrumming nearby, in the ceiling corners they made a sound like a headache. Loose greenery was growing through hairline cracks in the wall, the colour too vivid for this room.

The man nodded, satisfied. "Keep your peace, that's what I wanted to tell you. Just keep your peace for now."

He gave James a new set of clothes, trousers and a loose shirt, faded black.

"What is this place?" James asked.

"Once it was a school," the man said.

James waited for him to continue. The man just looked at him, tranquil, silent.

That night, the rains started. The grass in the wall dripped tiny beads of water. James felt unbearably cold. He remembered, one weekend, taking his brother to the Pacific Ocean. They had caught the ferry across the Strait of Georgia, and then driven the old Datsun to the western edge of Vancouver Island, through the shamelessly fat trees with their towering canopies. His brother, ten years younger, always wanted to hear about Tokyo, but James had little to say. He remembered the bomb shelters and the charred dog he saw once, and the brief sojourns home his father made, and how the war in China had sculpted his father into someone both powerful and empty. His brother waited patiently and James just shrugged and said, "Fuck Japan." The bottom of the Datsun was rusted through and the floor on the front passenger side had a magnificent hole, you could see the asphalt blurring by: drop something and it was gone forever. How many things had they lost to that gaping hole? His house keys, Hiroji's plastic watch, apples tumbling from their grocery bags, all sorts of rubbish.

"But one day you'll take me to Tokyo, right, and show me things."

"Show you what?" James had said, shrugging. "I'll introduce you to the girls I knew when I was four."

He could smell the sea through that hole long before they got there, the salt heaviness, the fresh green-ness of it. He loved the ocean no matter how desperately cold it was. He'd bought a wetsuit, a used one (he'd had no money for a new one) because he was addicted to the fury of the tide. Those currents knocked him back, they overpowered him, and yet he felt alive, not fragmented, not broken. He tried to explain this to Hiroji when they lay, that first night, in their one-season tent.

"It's religious," he had said finally, lacking words.

Hiroji said, "I like it too."

In the narrow glow of the flashlight, Hiroji's face was round and small.

James wanted to tell him, "I'm not your father. You don't have to look at me like that. You can yell at me and tell me I'm a fake."

Instead he said, "You didn't pack your schoolbooks, did you?"

Hiroji looked at him nervously. "Just a few."

"I'm going to lock them in the Datsun."

"Ha ha," his brother said.

"Ha ha," James answered.

The rain started. It drummed the ocean, it slipped through the high canopy of trees and reached their tent, a tapping of needles.

"Ichiro," his brother said tentatively. "Do we need to sleep in the car?"

"No, brother," James said. "It's fine. I chose a good place for us." James reached his fingers up and touched the tent walls, they were heavy with moisture, rain filling up all the pores, soon the wet would force its way through.

"Just close your eyes and get some sleep. The light will wake us early tomorrow."

"Okay," his brother said. "Okay, James."

He felt, sometimes, like Hiroji's father, as if the best part of his youth had already gone by. But these moments were fleeting. James was only seventeen after all, he was just a kid.

It rained all night. Sometimes he heard voices floating through the schoolhouse, he heard trucks stalling in the mud outside. James knew they would come for him in the middle of the night, slash his throat, and push his body into a pit before he was even alert enough to be afraid. He didn't want to die in the unthinking mud. He couldn't let this happen because there were people relying on him. There was Sorya and the promises he had made.

Kwan, this stranger, came to him in the shape of his brother and leaned his body against the far wall. His black hair fell forward over his eyes, his skin was the colour of cedar, he had thin lips and high, faint eyebrows. Every movement he made was precise, as if wasted movement itself was a crime, like spilled water in a time of drought. Kwan had Hiroji's watchful eyes. He was the opposite of James, he was not reckless or weak or self-pitying. Kwan took his time because he knew that the seconds were precious, doing the right thing in the right moment, every single time, was the only thing that could save him.

He studied Kwan and remembered his kid brother, the way Hiroji never spoke out of turn, never spoke without some prodding. If you didn't know him as James did, you would have thought that Hiroji was a bit slow, a bit dull, but really he was constantly rearranging things in his mind, he was opening and filing the information as it arrived, rather than letting it overflow and become meaningless. Yes, his brother was careful and he had been that way even when he was small. In the corner of the room, Hiroji, or was it Kwan or was it some meta-morphosis of the two or was it James as he once was, the James that might have grown up in Tokyo with a father and a language of his own, with a box in his heart to hide his fear, shifted his weight and knelt on the ground so now they could see each other clearly, on the same level. The boy studied him. There was one man in this room and one ghost. When James woke at the next knocking on the door, it was still pouring, rain was running thinly across the floor, cupping the light all to itself.

"Kwan?" the man's voice said.

James made no answer.

"Kwan?"

James reached out and plucked the weeds growing through cracks, he ate them and drank, foolishly, the dirty groundwater. Eventually, he heard the sound of the man's rubber sandals on the concrete landing, walking away. James's clothes were wet and they stank of the earth outdoors.

There's a room full of injured people and it brims with rot and excrement. The man brings James here in the middle of the night but what the hell is he supposed to do with no drugs, no nothing, barely even light to work by. He throws his hands up in frustration but the man doesn't seem to get it, he just watches expectantly as if James is Jesus with forty loaves at his beck and call. Forty ampoules. If James resists he'll get them all killed. He has no choice but to clean the wounds, dress them with scraps of cloth torn from the patients' own clothing, with wet cardboard or their filthy, multi-purpose kramas. He thinks in detail about his brother, his mother, and no one seems to notice his tears, a liquid, he believes, that is rich in painkillers. He attempts to clean the broken skin with the salinity of the fluid.

Sometimes the patients are Khmer Rouge cadre and sometimes they are prisoners who are only being prepared for the next round of interrogation. Before, in Canada, he never wondered how many deaths we can survive, how many deaths we can bear, how many deaths we deserve. He doesn't know what to do with the children who have become as blank-eyed as the adults.

A blade of morning light falls in between the wall and the ceiling. The man, they call him Chorn, escorts James back to the storeroom. Before he leaves, the man orders in a bowl of rice soup.

"Good night, Kwan," Chorn says through the locked door. James doesn't answer. On the floor, beside his food, is a letter. It is a single, lined page torn from a notebook. He recognizes Sorya's handwriting long before he deciphers the Khmer words. The letter is bare of details. It is written to him. She must be here, in Cambodia, somewhere. She did not escape to Bangkok. Sorya writes, *They told me that you are safe. That you survived.*

When Chorn returns at nightfall, James says, "What is this?" He has to control every word or they will overflow and hurt him. He says again, "What is this?"

"I can bring you a letter now and then. This is all I can do."

The words don't make sense to James. They don't tell him how the letter got here, or what it means. He picks up the sheet of paper, turns it over, looks for the information that is missing.

"Can you bring her?"

"That depends," the man says.

James takes a breath and the fetid air sinks sharply into his lungs. "You want to make every one of us small. Every one of us like you. Is that it?"

Chorn says nothing, he closes his eyes. He has a sharp face, a beak of a nose, and long, dark lashes, he has an armoured quiet that nothing James understands can penetrate.

"Listen," Chorn says. His voice is low and the words come so fast, they seem to evaporate as soon as he speaks. "Listen. I'm trying to help you. There is no other way. You want to know what we need from you? Everyone has to work. That's all. It's simple. There is no divide any longer between work and life, between life and death, between you and the world, between the world and Angkar. If you act correctly, you are the enemy, if you act incorrectly, you are the enemy. These are Angkar's own words. Can't you see that I'm trying to help you? A long time ago you were my friend. Don't you remember?"

James falters. He says, "You can protect her."

Chorn shakes his head. There's emotion on his face, like a mask that keeps slipping, that he pushes into place or removes at will. James is staring straight into his eyes and the man looks down.

"You still don't understand," Chorn says. "Unless you understand, we will both be accused. Not just her, but you and I as well. In Phnom Penh, you protected me. I never forgot."

James tries to wipe the fog, the dust, from his thoughts.

"How did you get this letter? Explain it to me."

"I have all the paper," Chorn says, lifting his hands, opening his fingers. "All the paper in this district, all the files, are here."

Chorn touches James's shoulder and the shock of the gesture blinds him awake.

"She made a mistake," Chorn says slowly, as if he is explaining himself to a child. "Her letters to you are a crime. She should never have tried to reach you. But, now, it's too late to help her. She has been revealed to the authorities."

James is not forced to work in the fields. He is not forced to do anything but wait. He hears a lot of things through the walls and what he hears is so chilling he believes, thought by thought, that he is a monster, that his mind is deforming. There was a woman in this prison. She was born in Phnom Penh but had gone away to study in France. She returned, a doctor also, to serve the country because she believed in the Khmer Rouge and a free

Cambodia. The Khmer Rouge caught her in her home village, along with her family, and this woman was arrested and accused. After several days, she wrote her first confession, tortured into writing, claiming, that she was a CIA spy. Tonight an ox-cart came and took her away to a different jail. James had helped prepare her for the journey and he saw her wounds, he saw the sadism of her interrogators, the ruptures on her skin. He wanted to tell her to succumb to her madness because madness is an escape, temporary or permanent, from this. From herself. But it was forbidden to exchange a word. He heard the ox-cart leave, turning up the earth, stuttering over the broken path, and the torturers laughing and saying their goodbyes. He saw this woman's face.

Sometimes, Chorn brings him outside, but only at night, only when all is still. A vitamin deficiency is causing his vision to blur so that when he looks up the stars all seem to be falling. Another letter comes a few weeks after the first, also delivered by Chorn. *I'm afraid,* she has written. *Every day I wonder if you will come. What should I do? They are watching me all the time.*

He asks for paper, for a pen. He begs for help.

"I am very sorry," the man says. "You cannot. It is far too dangerous."

James feels his entire body sickening. "Then you must tell her to stop writing."

The man shakes his head, frustrated. "Do you think it is up to me?"

"For god's sake, I'm begging you. Tell her to stop writing."

They left him alone all day. This is when you lie in the water, when you lie down on the shore of the Pacific and the tide comes in and you have to let it take you. You have to go. You belong to no one, Angkar says, and no one belongs to you, not your mother or your child or the woman you would give your life for. Families are a disease of the past. The only creature under your care is you: your hands, your feet, the hair on your head, your voice. Attachment is what will expose you as a traitor to the revolution, to the change that is coming, that is here. Attachment to the world is a crime. For too long, the people have suffered. For too long they have waited, but their desire is as great as the sea, as thirsty as the dry land. Even the rivers are cruel.

He pictured her in detail, her face, her mouth, her stillness. He begged her, in his mind, to stop writing, he wrote his letters to her on the wall of the store room, on the tiled floor. It's a trap, he told her. It's a goddamned trap.

He received another letter: *My love. They told me that you are near. They promised to bring you to me and I gave them all the money. I will keep trying to reach you, no matter the consequences. I want to bring about another future, the one I carried in my head for so long, all through the war.*

He started to weep and he couldn't stop. "Help her," James said. "Hide her somewhere. Bring her here."

Chorn looked at James. "The truth is," he said quietly, shamefully, "there is no James. I have never known this person James."

"Then tell her that he's dead. Tell her it's useless to write."

Chorn removed a straw bag that was hanging from his shoulder, and from the bag he withdrew bandages, pills, antibiotics, brandy, dressings, even a stethoscope.

It was fucked up, it was unbelievable. It couldn't be.

"All this suffering," Chorn said, "is for something. You don't know what this country was like before. You have to trust me." The man held on to the supplies as if they were religious objects, promises.

He must be hallucinating. He rubbed his hands over the cement tiles. "She didn't do anything wrong," James said. "I didn't do anything wrong."

"Only a dictator or an idiot would make that claim," Chorn said. He looked at the ground, at his toes protruding from his worn-down sandals, at the trail of dust he had brought into the already dusty room.

Chorn said in his quiet, detached way, "Angkar knows about James. But it does not know about Kwan. You see how I have tried to help you? Because some of us have many tricks, some of us have many names. There are people who are loyal only to me, but even I know the limits of what is possible. Look at this," he said, shaking the pills the way a mother might try to distract her baby. "Look what I found. There is still so much that we can do. Everyone had a different life before but it doesn't mean we must all go to the same end.

"Would you find it hard to believe," Chorn said, "that once, long ago, I was a monk? They came to the temple and they took all the children away. They went and made us into something else."

Before, when Dararith was still alive, the three of them had taken the motorcycle to Kep and they had stayed a week on the seaside. The ocean comes into this storeroom and covers it like a drawing. He can see the tide taking morsels of the land, bit by bit, away. That week, Dararith had disappeared for three days, he'd met a French girl with long, wavy hair, he'd offered to take her photograph with his brand-new Leica, but really it was Dararith who should've been the model. He was a handsome man with romantic eyes and full lips, a mysterious, colonial sexiness that made the women foolish. In contrast, James was a bore, or at least that's what Sorya told him, teasingly, looking past him to the sea.

"And what about you?" he'd asked in English. "If I wanted to take your picture?"

"I'm the true photographer," she had answered in Khmer.

"Take your brother's camera, then."

"I tried!" she said, laughing. "Believe me, I tried. But Dararith, he uses it to meet women, it's only a toy for

him, whereas I know I'm a photographer. If only someone would give me a chance."

"What would you shoot?"

"Once I took a picture of my students at the lycée."

He never knew whether she was serious or joking.
He was a buffoon, a hippopotamus, sitting beside her.

"I'm your friend, aren't I?" she had said on the last
night that he saw her.

"Am I being demoted?"

"You're my best friend," she had said, "and you
don't really know it. You don't value it."

He'd felt belittled. He had wanted to raise his voice:
I'm in love with you, is that such a small thing? I've
loved you since the day I met you, why is that worth
so little? Now he wonders how he misunderstood her
so badly. How stupid, how arrogant was he, that he
couldn't persuade her to leave for Bangkok, pride had
made him unforgivably blind. He'd wanted her to wait
for him. In his heart, he'd wanted this, to prove something, because they had both been alone. They had already left their families even before Angkar came. They
only had each other.

"Tell me about Tokyo," she had said, just like Hiroji.
They were like two birds pecking at his head. On the
southern borders of the city, rockets were falling. They
could see the fighting, like sheaves of fire.

"There's nothing much to tell."

"They bombed it very badly, didn't they?"

"It was Dante's fifth circle."

"I used to teach that poem," she said. "I taught, 'Through me is the way to the sorrowful city, through me is the way to the lost people.'"

"Admit it, you have a lover somewhere, don't you?" he said lightly, wanting to turn the darkness aside. "A boy much nicer than me."

"I'm twenty-six years old," she said. "Everyone around me is married with ten children. I live in a city that's about to fall to the Khmer Rouge. What can I possibly know about love?"

"Come with me to Neak Luong. Come tomorrow."

She shook her head.

"Take this money and buy us two tickets for Bangkok."

"Honestly, you want to leave Phnom Penh? This heaven."

"Do you?"

She smiled at him, she folded her sadness away. "All this time, I only stayed because of you."

The sea, the sea. The words ran in his mind, the future his father had once envisioned, the promises he had kept before he died.

"Some things don't end," she said, kissing his lips. "We both knew, didn't we? From the very beginning. I knew. You would be the one I loved."

What did he say? He had only kissed her. He had treated everything as if it were ephemeral, as if things could only be beautiful if they were passing, if they were mortal. "Can you hear me," she had whispered one night, thinking he was asleep. He had kept his eyes closed. All those months, he had put on such a show of being brave, he had made a joke of his needs. He had wanted to please her, to keep her, and he didn't know how.

He sleeps on the cement tiles, in the prison, segregated from everyone else because he is useful to Chorn. Sometimes the man comes and sits with him. Sometimes he brings a grandchild or a daughter and James gives them medicine, he cleans a wound, he works according to the tasks he is given. His own body is unrecognizable, it is a parody of a human being, mere bones, dark shadows where muscle used to be. Kwan sits in the corner and day by day grows stronger, Kwan feeds memories to James, experiences that are part James, part Dararith and Sorya, part Hiroji, part Chorn. King James is a useless army of invisible men, of stories given and received like bread on the communion line, and it's the only bread he has to keep him going. King James is a rotten child, he's losing his mind and also his sight. Piece by piece, day by day, Kwan is taking over, and James is tired now, but he hangs on like a cat at the table because any scrap could be the one that saves him. He dreams of Sorya in the daytime, but never at night. Water seeps down the walls, along the green lines of invading grass, dribbling down to the ground.

Chorn goes away for many days, and a child, blind in one eye, brings the food. When Chorn returns, sick-looking, he asks James, "Do you know anything about planting rice? About crops?"

James shakes his head. "But when I was a teenager, I worked one summer in the forest, I felled trees." It was in Port Hardy, on the northern cusp of Vancouver Island, a job found for him by his mother's hairdresser. He had learned to swagger in that isolated logging town and give off the impression of solidity.

Chorn looks at him, skeptical. "With an axe?"

"Sometimes."

Chorn nods, pleased with this information. They sit quietly, and Chorn drums his fingertips against his knees. His hands are pale, as if, outdoors in the drenching sun, he keeps them safely hidden in his pockets.

"What's it like now?" James asks, breaking the stillness. "In the cities."

Chorn waits, without responding, without looking at James, as if Chorn, too, is expecting another person to answer. In the pause, there's the hard melody of an ox-bell, the only music James has heard in too long, and it seems to stretch like a physical object through the air and knock against the walls of the room.

"Everything is very organized," Chorn says. "They are making an archive in which nothing is missing. Every person must write a biography. They must write it many times to ensure that all the details are correct."

He prays his hands together to stop the drumming. "Phnom Penh is very still. In fact, it is empty. Every movement you make is like the first one ever made. I thought I was the only one alive. In the market, where the vendors used to be, there are small trees growing. Less than a year but already the jungle has arrived, it is threatening to strangle everything else.

"They have thousands and thousands of files. I delivered my share as well. I had to sign my name many times because they are terrified of missing pieces. Many times I signed my name." Chorn runs his hand over his mouth, closes his eyes, and nods. James feels as cold as the walls. "They put me in an apartment. A family's apartment. There were plates on the table, but the food had rotted. The owner collected stamps. Some were framed on the walls. I was standing there, looking at them, when the telephone rang. I went into the kitchen and the telephone kept ringing and ringing, I thought if I answered I would be punished, I was convinced it was a trap so I just stood there and waited, without moving, I waited for it to stop. Like a child.

"Somebody's photos were sitting there, in the room, in picture frames. I don't know why, but I put one in my pocket. A photograph of a woman. She reminded me of my oldest sister. Do you remember her? You always thought she was pretty."

Chorn looks up, an embarrassed half-smile on his lips. "They are making an archive in which everything is accounted for, and once a file is there, it is eternal. This is Angkar's memory. We are all writing our histories for Angkar."

Chorn pauses and in the gap, James says, "What happened to your sister?"

He doesn't answer. Instead he says, "Listen."

The change happens so fast, James doesn't quite trust his eyes, Chorn's expressions come and go as quickly as a change in light. Chorn looks past him and James thinks that, finally, after all these months, he is about to be accused. Of what crime? It hardly matters. All the sentences are the same.

"This woman, Sorya. She had a child."

Seconds go by but the words don't mean anything. It's a game, James thinks. It's yet another one of his sadistic games. They used to do this when they were young, tell each other stories. Once he ran home and told his mother that Hiroji had been hit by a car. He had wanted to test her, and he remembers now the strange satisfaction he took from the agony of her cries.

Chorn says, "Maybe we're at the end now. There are purges everywhere. One hundred people, five hundred people. Soon we won't be alone, even here. The Centre is moving, you see. Angkar is running from itself, but it is meeting itself in every corner. Meeting all its enemies. Do you understand what I'm telling you? I have children too. I have children I want to save. I tried to find a name. Someone told me Dararith. I couldn't ask more without attracting attention. But they told me Sorya named the boy Dararith."

The air in the room is stagnant, like a pool of black water into which they are both sinking. It's Kwan who finds the words, who asks the next question. It isn't James, James is falling down.

"Did you keep her here? Was Sorya at this prison?"

"No," the man says.

"Was she here?"

Kwan gets up from the corner. He comes so near to them, James can hear him breathing, this exhalation in his head. Chorn is looking straight at him, but Chorn's face is closed, muting all the clues. Only his hands give him away, their immobility, their held breath. His hands are a lie. Was it possible that all this time his hands were a lie?

"You're my friend," Chorn tells him. "Why can't you understand? I'm giving you this information because you are my friend."

"Why did they kill her?"

Chorn shakes his head, visibly upset. "I don't know. Maybe she didn't die. Don't talk about this. Lower your voice."

But then he reaches into his pocket and he takes out Sorya's letters, five of them, creased and beginning to tear. He sets them on the floor and, for the first time, looks straight into James's eyes.

"Why are you doing this?" James says. He is nauseated and the man is breaking apart in his vision.

"Let her go. The past is done."

The man stands up and dust comes off him, it sticks to the air. James wonders why he doesn't stand up, push Chorn backwards, crack the weight of his skull against the cement wall, spill this man's life onto the once-elegant tiles, into the black water, go to be tortured and executed for a crime he can truly understand. His thoughts are viscous and slow. He could stand up now and find some strength, take this because there is nothing left to take. So what if Angkar is everywhere, he could kill this one man and be done with it here, he could choke his own weakness.

The door scrapes closed. James opens his eyes.

A shadow comes and sits in front of him and James can't help himself, his head drops forward against his brother's chest. He can feel the bones there, his brother is skinny, still a boy, but he is stronger and more complete than James will ever be. He cannot bring himself to touch the letters, they sit on the tiled floor too lightly. The ox-bell has stopped ringing and now a voice is speaking urgently. Prodding the animal forward. Hours pass. Days fall down, maybe it is a month that he sits like this, or just a few days, eating and sleeping and wasting away, remembering everything. Her watchful face, her scent, her hands pushing him back. No matter what the voice says, the animal won't move. There is water everywhere, he cries until all the rest comes out, all of it spills onto his ragged shirt, onto the tiled floor, and seeps into the cracks that lead out of the store room. There is no wind in this room, no oxygen. Where is emptiness? No matter where he goes, he can't find emptiness.

"Do you believe him?" Kwan asks.

James, wherever he is, trickling across the ground, spreading down to the lowest places, says no.

"No," Kwan says. "Okay, James. Okay. Let go."

"I can't, I can't. I can hear her."

"Don't listen."

"I promised to bring her to the sea."

"Let go, brother."

"I promised her."

"Let go."

❖

The last letter comes to him much later. He is standing at the Laos–Cambodia border and it is 1981, two years since the Khmer Rouge was defeated. In all that time, James, now known as Kwan – a mute, a smuggler, and a solitary man – has heard the most remarkable stories: the people who have been recovered, the strange ways in which children were protected, the objects returned to their owner's hands. He hears them at each and every encounter, when he trades the sugar and salt he has carried on his back from Thailand. The stories are repeated so often, they change into fairy tales of the most devastating kind.

In 1980, he went back to their apartment on Monivong Boulevard. There was a family living there, one of those new Cambodian families consisting of orphans: a man and woman with someone else's children, a friend turned uncle, a stray niece. They had traded everything of value in the apartment but they had held on to the photographs, without the frames, which they kept together in a blue plastic bag. Kwan gave them one precious U.S. dollar and came away with photos of Sorya and Dararith, and of James. The stray niece came running after him and asked if she could keep the plastic bag, so now the photos stay in his shirt pocket, held to the fabric with a paper clip.

Chorn was right. This is the city of before. Five-year-olds fending for themselves, and the Khmer Rouge, arrogant, shit-faced, still prideful in their stronghold in the north, still holding their seat at the United Nations and hobnobbing with the Western elite, conspiring to take it back. Phnom Penh is no longer the agitated city he remembers, no, the dial has ticked back and stripped the place of people and goods, it is a city now where the kids run naked, where people walk around with photographs of missing family, where, by accident, you step into a pile of bones, rinse your foot off, and then move on, where men and women dress in hothouse colours, clashing motifs, to push back the memory of black clothes and black hearts. Those barbarians had sawed off the hands of the ancient Buddhas and thrown them into the water, now the children fish them up and stack them on the riverside and try to sell them to the aid workers or the off-duty Vietnamese. Other, more terrible losses, come up from the mud.

He went to Kampot, riding on the back of a moped driven by a ten-year-old who had stolen it from who knows where. This ten-year-old is so wizened, he doesn't smile or laugh or anything. He just names, matter-of-factly, the price, U.S. dollars or Thai baht, no other currency accepted. When the boy takes the cash in his bony fingers, he chews his lip and studies the bills, already assessing the things he has to buy. What a bombed-out ruin Kampot is now, buildings made unstable by the shelling, buildings that look like someone kicked them in the knee-caps, hard. In his youth, Kwan drove a lorry so he knows these roads well, but still it's a shock to see the devastation and how the sea just keeps rolling in, unstoppable.

"Cigarettes," the kid demands.

Kwan shakes his head.

"You can speak now," the kid says abruptly. "Angkar is done. Finished."

Kwan gestures that he can't speak, he has never spoken.

The kid shrugs, folds the bills up, tucks them somewhere in his pants. "My name's Joe," he says, mangling the word. "You need anything, you ask for Joe." He revs the accelerator, the engine hacks, and he wobbles away over the cracked street.

That night, sitting on a mound of stones, he hears someone playing music on a record player. A man calls out the name Sorya and he lifts his head and sees a thin woman dancing slowly, her wrists turning in the same way they must have done decades ago, when she was a girl and this was Indochina and the French swanned down the wide boulevards and hid their guilt in a veil of opium smoke. Khmer dance is its own language, this is what Dararith had once explained: "This gesture means you have come across a flower, a lotus, and you are offering it, and this gesture here means love. And this gesture is water."

"Water, water, everywhere," Sorya had said. "Come and dance with me, Dararith. Nothing so classical. Just the *ramvong*. Just the lindy hop."

"Wait," Dararith had said. "Let me take your photo."

"Click away," she said.

Here she is now, in his pocket.

He had felt, at the time, lonely: an outsider watching these two siblings, this self-sufficient love. But he knows now there are no outsiders. There is no walking away at the end, delusion has to finish somewhere, it has to end or else weakness will outlast them all. He has to commit to something or be done. From Kampot he travels to the prison where Chorn, too, was eventually arrested, eventually tortured and killed. In the storeroom where he passed nearly two years, boxes are rotting in the heat, files and pages, confusions, accusations. He went through them and found the sixth letter, the last one, the same thin weight of paper, but her handwriting had deteriorated, the pen had hardly any ink. Who was she writing to? Not James anymore, or not just James. *They are throwing us away*, she wrote, *and I can't understand why because all I wanted was for the war to end, no matter who won. I never admitted any allegiance. My name is Sorya. I am the sister of Dararith, the daughter of Kravann and Mary, the wife of James. I was a teacher.* There was a biography and a confession, and in the biography was the name of their son, just as Chorn had told him. The prison file had dates, but no date of death, there was not even a photograph, there was no file for the baby, and he dared to believe that they had been absolved. That she wandered, like him, with a different name and a new soul.

Everyone is searching. Everyone is looking into every passing face and wondering if the next person along the road will be the beloved, the dreamed of. Maybe this life is the dream. If gods existed, he would still be waking up to the sound of her moving through the apartment. Here she is now, coming into the room to wake him. Here she is.

"I'm a selfish Buddhist," she had told him once. "Something of me will return, something will come around and around forever, but it won't be Sorya. I have only this one chance."

He travelled on, chasing a rumour of Dararith, to the Laos–Cambodian border where caves slip into one country and out the other. He, too, had hidden here for several months after running away from his work unit, they had been cutting trees in the forest when he attacked the lone cadre and left him for dead. Now he hardly remembers that he killed a boy. It is difficult to move during the rainy season. He can guess the date of his son's birthday. Small children, he knows, were sent to America, to France, they took flight to places he can't imagine, or they persevered, here, like Joe. They sold things or sometimes they sold themselves. The jungle has invaded the cities but now the hungry people are cutting it back. They are skinning the trees again and eating the bark. From place to place he defaces the walls with a black marker, Khmer words, Khmer letters: Sorya Dararith James. You can follow the trail but you can't know in which direction you are headed, down to the end, or reversing, forever, to the beginning.

Hiroji

❖

Monday, March 6
[fragment]

It is April 1976. A burning hot day and the sky so delicate a blue, the white sun will surely burn the colour
off. Hiroji should have sunglasses but he lost them in a
Bangkok government office where an official with con-
cerned eyes hid them under an airmail envelope, dis-
tracting Hiroji with instructions to another border
town, where the sixth and hopefully final permit could
be obtained. He should have said something, he should
have snuck his hand under the envelope and retrieved his
sunglasses, but he didn't. He could only sit, dazed by the
heat and the man's shy audacity, and watch.

Now, a half-dozen permits later and several months
gone by, he stands on the Thai side of the border and stares
across a narrow river into Cambodia. When Phnom Penh
fell to the Khmer Rouge, the airport was in ruins. A year
later, and it hasn't reopened. There's been no word from
his brother in all that time, not a letter, not a clue. James
has been wheeled into another room but the room itself

has disappeared. On the opposite bank, the Cambodian side, blistered grass unrolls, folding up into stark mountains. The heat is dizzying. He shifts his feet on the dry ground, blinks the sweat from his eyes, and tries to comprehend what he's seeing. A black-clothed boy, the Khmer Rouge guard, stands alert at the end of a one-lane bridge, his Kalashnikov leaning against his fingertips, barrel up. The border is eerily quiet and then, abruptly, gunfire sounds. Khmer Rouge soldiers arrive. They gaze disdainfully across the border, at Hiroji. When they depart, one remains, like a black feather fallen from the crow.

Soon the rainy season will arrive and it will be nearly impossible to travel in the flooding. Even James won't be able to manage it. Hiroji paces the border. In his head, he adds up his expenses: how much cash he needs to stay another month, another two months. How much for a lift to the next refugee camp, from Sa Kaeo to Aran, and farther north. Fees and living expenses for September, when he must return to university. The return flight, all his bills. He paces until the sun has burned a headache deep behind his eyes. It's a twenty-minute walk back to Aranyaprathet, a long walk through wrinkled scrub and gnarled trees, behind tin shacks, beside military trucks that shake the road and heave the dust up. He walks slowly because he is still not used to the heat. In all his life, he has never felt so powerless.

—

Aranyaprathet smells of overripe pineapples and mangy dogs. Beside his guesthouse, a shrill, dead-eyed woman tries to sell him Buddha heads. She scratches at him with her fingernails, tugs at his clothes, alternately whispers and barks at him until, finally, he chooses one, a sleepy bodhisattva with its eyes half-open, cold against his fingertips, too light for this world. The old woman clucks reassuringly, scratching the bills together, she drums them on the surrounding objects, holds the money up against her forehead, smiles generously.

Upstairs, inside his room, he sets the bodhisattva on the desk, inside the square of sunshine floating through the window. He removes, from his shirt pocket, two colour photographs of James, damp from his sweat, and lays them on the desk to dry. Hiroji sits on the edge of the bed, thinks of making tea, thinks of calling his mother, thinks of an empty stairwell in the School of Medicine at the University of British Columbia, the carpet of grass out front, where he used to read and watch the girls go by. Objects in the hotel room begin to disconnect from one another, first the mirror turns away, then the table stutters toward the door, then the walls come apart. The bodhisattva falls face down as if to kiss the earth, he's so tired and he hasn't slept in days. Hiroji blinks his eyes. It's his birthday, today or tomorrow depending on the time zone, and he wonders if the party (the non-existent party) will bring him gifts or money, plans for the future, or just fond memories.

A rattling at the door bothers him. He watches the knob turn of its own accord, the door jumps open and a face appears at the level of the table: furtive eyes, a heavy frown. The Cambodian boy, Nuong, comes into the room, exhales a jumble of Khmer words. His flickering hands clutch his stomach.

"I'm sorry," Hiroji says, ashamed. "I lost track of time."

Nuong looks at him, wide-eyed and anxious.

"Okay. Let's go." Hiroji returns the photographs to his shirt pocket and they descend. Nuong, hunched like a shrivelled leaf, hurries quickly along the road.

At their regular place, they step through a windowless wall, drop down onto red plastic chairs. A long-faced man brings them two bowls of noodles, they arrive in a bouquet of steam. Hiroji removes his glasses and lays them, arms open, on the table. It's crowded in the restaurant this morning. Men in undershirts snap their newspapers back, hold them high like flags. The regulars nod at him: Thai Red Cross and USAID workers, gamblers, black market profiteers, foreign service officers, stringers for AP, AFP, Reuters, stringers as the conscience of the world, here for a few days before pulling out. The owner has a bird in a bamboo cage, the cage covered by a thin sarong. The bird chortles in its private darkness.

Hiroji closes his eyes, rubs the dust and wetness from them. He isn't upset, just tired, but Nuong, his mouth bursting with noodles, stares at Hiroji in shocked sadness.

"Allergies. I have allergies," Hiroji says, even though the boy doesn't understand much English.

To trick the sadness from Nuong's eyes, he pushes his food toward the boy. Nuong accepts. In minutes, the noodles are gone.

"They won't confiscate your food," Hiroji says, but the boy just looks up at Hiroji expectantly.

After lunch, Hiroji stops in at the makeshift Red Cross office, where a terse woman his mother's age operates the Xerox machine, telling him, as it spits out posters, that his bill is running high and he should clear his account, then she disappears behind a stubble of folders. He takes the posters out of the machine. By the time he carries them outside, the sheets are already moist from the sweat on his hands.

James's face smiles out from Aranyaprathet's bulletin board where the locals come to read the daily newspapers, James smiles from all the downtrodden shacks along the road toward the border, Hiroji keeps going until he runs out of posters, and then he turns back to see the sheets dancing along the road, Nuong running back and forth to gather them up. Cheap glue. The ink fades fast in this climate and he'll do it all over again next week, this is what he tells himself and it works, it makes his heart slow down, it calms his hands.

Back at the Red Cross, Hiroji stations himself at the telephone. He calls the Cambodian Ministry of the Interior, he lets the line ring fifty, sixty times before giving up. He telephones the Cambodian Foreign Ministry in Paris, a man with a delicate voice answers, puts him on hold, and then the line goes dead.

The Xerox woman tells him there are a dozen refugees newly arrived in the south, near Mairut. "Take a moto-taxi," she says. "Better yet, ask our driver to take you."

Hiroji stares at the map and absent-mindedly fingers the cash in his pocket.

"Okay," he says. "Tomorrow."

The heat is surreal. Hiroji walks back to the border, stares across the river, wonders if the Khmer Rouge soldier will suddenly vacate his post, if some door will swing open, if people will rush out as he rushes in. Cambodia is right there, right in front of him, as accessible as a landscape painting. But chip off the paint and there's a dirty, yawning hole. His thoughts are melting. *James needs you*, he thinks. He tries to think of someone else he can appeal to, a diplomat, a fixer.

James is waiting, he tells himself again. But when his brother finally does come home, what will he do? Will he disappear again, like he used to after binge drinking at some forgotten dive in Chinatown. Even blind drunk, his brother could walk a straight line, tell a joke and remember the punchline, advise Hiroji to stay a kid because a kid's life is the best life, the bee's knees.

"I'm not a kid," he had protested.

"Dream on, brother. Let's go for a drive."

It was Hiroji who had steered them through the wet nights, while James pushed his tipsy head out the window, toward Lion's Gate Bridge, toward the sea-swept darkness of the north. Once they went all the way to Squamish, they rolled the windows down and listened to the tide, admired the teenaged girls sitting on the picnic tables. "Japs," one said and the other girl giggled. "Sayonara!" They smiled at Hiroji enticingly.

"One for you and one for me," his brother slurred. Then James closed his eyes as if the darkness was too bright. Hollow beer bottles clinked together, the girl's voices pitched and rolled like the tide coming in.

"James," Hiroji said when the beach was empty. "Can I drive us home now?"

"Sure, brother. Drive away. I might take a snooze."

Hiroji swung the door open.

"Do you remember Dad?" James said, collapsing into the front seat.

He hesitated before answering. "Not so much."

"That's good," James said. "That's okay. That's what he would have wanted, that's what we all want, isn't it? Hey, world! Turn a blind eye to my misdeeds."

Hiroji just drove, uncomprehending.

Every week now he tracks down government offi-cials who nod sympathetically, who shake his hand and tell him, frankly, there's nothing to be done. He goes to sleep thinking about the covered birds and wakes up, the air close, smelling of mud. Once, Hiroji saw Nuong cooking strands of meat. He had killed a cat, skinned it, and roasted it. "If you're hungry," Hiroji had said, pointing at the carcass and shaking his head, "why don't you tell me? Those animals could be diseased. They might make you sick." The boy had blinked in surprise.

"Try it," Nuong said in Khmer.

He watched the boy devouring the meat, sucking the marrow noisily and succinctly from the bones. The boy only rests in the afternoons. He lies down on Hiroji's bed, hands interlaced, studying the cracked ceiling.

"What should we call you," Hiroji had asked when they met, for the first time, in the medical tent. The boy had crouched on the bamboo mat, keeping his distance from the translator, a teenaged girl.

"Bruce Lee," Nuong said. "I am Bruce Lee."

"We walked through the forest," Nuong told him, his voice humming beneath the girl's. "We came up through the forest."

"Who?"

"Me and my brothers."

It costs Hiroji thirty dollars every week to bribe the Thai guard, but at least Nuong comes and goes freely from the camp where the UNHCR rations are only twenty cents per person, per day.

James calls to him from the other room: "You home, bro? Is that you?"

Hiroji holds his breath and doesn't answer.

His brother shrugs, "I had to live my life."

Back at the Red Cross office, Hiroji telephones his mother, trying to sound upbeat. "You've heard from Ichiro?" she asks, her voice wobbling with joy. "Not yet, but soon." Her disappointment leaves a cut in his heart. He tells her, impulsively, that he'll stay in Thailand another month, he will delay his studies. When he puts down the receiver it seems like the end of the world: the phone call cost forty-two U.S. dollars. He can live on dried noodles but what will he feed Nuong? Where will they sleep? He returns to his room but Nuong is gone. Hiroji lies down on the hard bed, watches the crooked turning of the fan. In his dreams that night, his brother offers him pastel-pink candies to make all the helpless thoughts go away, they taste like Pepto-Bismol. *Pepto-abysmal*, his brother says. He wakes up and knows that James is dead, there's nothing to be done, the vigil is over. He wakes up and it's his twenty-seventh birthday. Lightning stutters in the sky and the rains start again, raucous and temperamental. He can't accept it, he doesn't know whether to stay or leave, he wants to do right by James but he doesn't know how, he can't imagine how.

At dawn, unable to sleep, he dresses and slogs through the mud to the border. Nuong is there, incongruously, half-blotted out by the rain. The boy is nearly unrecognizable, his eyes are bugging out, he looks rabid. "Nuong," Hiroji says but the boy doesn't react to his name. On the other side of the bridge the Khmer Rouge guard lifts his Kalashnikov, lifts the goddamned thing so easily and swivels it so the barrel is facing forward. The rain is everywhere, obscenely loud, drumming against the frozen air. Nuong looks like he is about to run across the bridge, straight into the guard, deep into the minefields.

Nuong calls, in Khmer, "Are you going to shoot me?" His voice carries, both childlike and detached.

The guard on the other side makes no response.

"Will you shoot? Shoot, okay? Shoot."

From where Hiroji stands, the guard looks like a piece of smudged charcoal. Nuong takes a step forward. "Why don't you shoot?"

The guard picks up something from the ground, grips it in his right hand, and then flings it nastily across the river.

Nuong flinches. The rock flies through the rain, it clears the bridge but misses him.

Nobody says anything for a moment and then, slowly, Nuong walks to the foot of the bridge. The guard yells at him to get back. The rifle shakes as he raises his voice, high-pitched, stunned and enraged, and the rain seems to part around the gun. Nuong gets down on his hands and knees. He starts pawing at the mud. The guard keeps screaming. The torrent has softened all the edges so that the land and the boys are the same brown colour, the same weak consistency. Nuong stands up, holding something in his right hand. The guard lets off a hail of bullets. Still, nothing happens, it must be the heavy rain that is blurring things or maybe the guard is intentionally firing wide, but Nuong continues to stand there, drenched, holding what Hiroji can now see is a rock. The guard taunts Nuong to come forward, to throw it, to cross the bridge, to come home, come home, if you come home I'll give you everything you want, but the boy just stands there staring like a lost dog, a sick child.

At the guesthouse, Nuong takes off his wet clothes, lies down on the bed, and there is no emotion at all, just an extraordinary, disturbing stillness that Hiroji has never seen before in anyone. He had picked up the boy after he sat down in the mud, unmoving, and carried him back to Aran, piggyback style, as if they were a father and son coming home from the park on a Sunday afternoon.

He could feed this boy and defend him but there's a limit he finally perceives now, a limit to what Nuong will say and what he, Hiroji, will ever be able to understand. The boy has survived, he's turning into someone else, but all the broken edges are rubbing together and injuring him every time he moves.

Nuong opens his eyes and says, in English, that he's hungry.

They get up and walk to the restaurant.

Hiroji wants to ask him if there are any foreigners in the new Cambodia, if there are doctors there, and why so few people have escaped across the border. Are the stories of the refugees true? They say the cities are empty, that children are executed for missing their parents, that torture and killing are commonplace. The French newspapers are reporting that eight hundred thousand people died in the first year of the revolution alone. But how could he ask a child such a question, even if the child knows the answer?

At the restaurant, Nuong says insistently, "I'm hungry."

By the end of 1977, they are surrounded by scores of missionaries and aid workers, by reporters, spies, and swindlers. More shelters bubble up from the ground, more generators and supplies arrive, but it's never enough. He alternates between a dozen camps along the border, leaving Aranyaprathet for Lumpuk and Mairut, then threading back again. The shelters, blue tarpaulins hooked onto bamboo stakes, are overrun, polluted, and dank. Twice a month, he hitches a ride in the Red Cross truck, he returns from Bangkok with cases of tinned milk and dried noodles, with notebooks and pencils for Nuong, and he does the same things over and over again, asks the same people the same questions, Xeroxes more photographs of James, phones his mother. Over the decrepit lines, he tries to reassure her. She tells him not to give up hope.

The hills are completely green, the grass is technicolour, fruit falls everywhere and rots on the ground.

The boy draws unbelievable things.

The objects in the hotel room separate. Metallic paint chips off the bodhisattva's head.

Nuong says, in his precarious English, that he would like medicine. "What kind of medicine?" Hiroji asks, curious.

The boy just looks at him.

"What kind?" Hiroji asks again. "What kind?"

The boy cradles his head and stays in that position for a frighteningly long time.

Somewhere, now, a surgeon could burn a lesion into the boy's brain. It's possible to lessen Nuong's suffering if the boy accepts some degree of loss. They can turn down the volume on all his emotions, pinch the air out of his sadness, turn him dull and pure as snow. Hiroji has professors who say there is no suffering, there is only chemistry. Suffering is a description but chemistry is the structure. In any case, a pill can dampen some receptors, dim the lights a little. Surgery can make him care a little less. Pain and suffering are not, in the end, the same thing, one can be cleaved from the other like a diamond split along its planes, so that you feel pain but you are no longer bothered by it. He has seen a patient, huddling in a corner, at the mercy of a condition so devastating that even a slight breeze from the window would cause him unbearable suffering. After surgery, he told his doctors that the pain was exactly as it was, but he did not feel it as greatly. "It's as if," he had said, a cool blandness in his eyes, "the pain is not being done *to me*." One day, maybe in a ten years, or fifty years, a surgeon will be able to do this with disturbing precision, destroy a whirlpool of memory, an entire system of feelings, but in the meantime it's like taking a hatchet to a spider's web.

By early 1979, the border area is a dead-eyed, stinking hell. He signs on as an aid worker with the Red Cross and they give him a stipend and a room. In January, the Vietnamese Communists crossed the Cambodian border, swept the Khmer Rouge aside, and took Phnom Penh in less than two weeks. The refugees wash up in their black clothes, so debilitated and disturbed that Hiroji thinks he is walking through an exhumed cemetery, they are more soil and sickness than human beings. Orphaned children piled together in a cloud of flies, little girls who are a jigsaw of bones, numb parents. He volunteers with the Red Cross but the supplies are so limited he works in a state of heartless efficiency. It's the only way that he can cope. Film crews record a girl, the same age as Nuong, suffering from starvation. On camera, she dies. Rows of cork boards overflow with letters, queries, and pictures of the missing. He adds James's photograph but, within a day, it's covered over by other missing people. He falls asleep tasting flies in his mouth, he hallucinates dead women stuck to his shoes. Vancouver and the University might as well be drawn on paper, he begins to forget that other people don't live this way. *Bye-bye*, the children say, when they glimpse him arriving, walking, working, leaving. *Bye-bye!* He keeps James's photo in his pocket all the time but the shame he feels searching for his brother, this foreigner, one person out of two million, distresses him.

Nuong is sponsored, all of a sudden, by a family in the United States. The adoption, arranged by an American Christian relief agency, happens so fast Hiroji is caught off guard. He has to hide his unhappiness in a bloom of smiles. In a few weeks, Nuong will board a plane from Bangkok to Chicago, and then from Chicago to Lowell, Massachusetts. His new family sends him a greeting card with a snapshot of balloons. Nuong wants to know if he will be given food on the crossing, if Hiroji will visit him, if it is advisable to take everything with him, his books, pencils, and quietly accumulated stash of Nescafé, and not glance back over his shoulder, the way the Christian missionaries taught them, to prevent the salt from flowing back up through his mouth, out his nostrils. Hiroji doesn't know what to say, he doesn't understand this boy.

"Why are you so sad all the time?" Nuong asks him in his now-melodic English. "Is it so very bad where you come from?"

Hiroji has to laugh.

Nuong doesn't smile. He says, "Thank you heaven I am not going to Canada."

More refugees arrive every month, wasting, mangled bodies.

Hiroji makes a gift to Nuong of all his remaining money, which isn't a great deal, and the shining bodhisattva. He accompanies him as far as Bangkok and he tells Nuong to be strong, not to look back, to be brave.

The boy looks so small with his suitcase and his blunt haircut, wearing a knit sweater for the first time. He does what Hiroji says and he doesn't look back, he launches himself courageously up into the sky.

A few weeks later, Hiroji sits with his mother in the apartment he grew up in on the east side of Vancouver. Her hair has gone wiry and white, and the tea is pale because she has been re-using the same leaves too many times. They go through all the details ten times, a hundred times. She, too, makes lists. She smiles her old smile at him and asks when he will go back to Aranyaprathet.

"Soon," he says.

"Next month?"

"Soon."

After a week of this they both fall silent. He spends too many hours in the second bedroom, which is overflowing with their adolescent junk: deflated soccer balls, bottle collections, homework assignments, and the assorted dregs of childhood. In a biscuit tin, he finds James's birth certificate and an expired driver's licence, both with his brother's birth name, Junichiro Matsui. In each photo, James is grinning. He looks young, he looks careless, as if the days have no weight on him, as if he is higher up or better than all the rest. Hiroji shoves the ID into his backpack.

It is surprisingly easy to impersonate his brother and, each time he passes for James, he feels more in control, more at peace with himself. He gets a new driver's licence, opens a bank account, and deposits a small sum of money. The truth is, they don't really look alike, but Hiroji has a trustworthy disposition, people look at him and see an honest face. They seem glad to help. A month later, while attending a conference in Rome, Hiroji gets a fresh haircut and presents himself at the Canadian Embassy. Calmly, believing his own illusions, he tells the wary man behind the glass that his passport has been stolen and could he apply for a new one? He has a police report showing that he, Junichiro Matsui, had his briefcase stolen while visiting the Trevi Fountain. The hardnosed man barely looks at him: he takes Hiroji's falsified ID, photocopies it, and hands it back. Two weeks later, Hiroji signs for the passport of Junichiro Matsui. He buries it in his suitcase and tells himself that he is only preparing to meet James again, that these are necessary preparations for his brother's repatriation. On paper, his brother still exists, he still belongs to a country, a home.

Finally, he is able to enter Cambodia, flying in on a Red Cross plane with two French doctors who murmur the rosary.

It is mid-1979, months after the fall of the Khmer Rouge. All over the city, people are rebuilding their lives in the street. He sees old men cooking meals in front of the Royal Palace where gold shingles sparkle like the crests of the ocean, he sees girls who sleep in the rusted carcasses of tanks, in straw huts, in silken hammocks. Farther along, on Monivong Boulevard, a wide road shaded by blossoms, smashed cars are piled four, five high, in a kind of monumental fuck you to Mercedes. Heaps of refrigerators and sofas are degrading in the humidity, bourgeois comforts evicted from their homes and left to rough it out. A boy waits with a car jack slung across his chest, cradling it like a mini AK-47. Alert with insomnia, Hiroji wanders the city that hardly seems a city at all. The citizens are all sleeping outdoors, where they can see and hear in every direction. He passes Vietnamese patrols, women ringed by children, people on mats and sheets all along the pavement, no electricity but dozens of candles shivering in glass jars. People follow him, they ask him if he knows the man from UNHCR who promised to bring charcoal last week, or the technician from the factory who was supposed to repair the sewing machines, or the doctor who ran out of bandages but said he would be back. Hiroji cannot bring himself to say that these experts have already flown out. All the Western aid is at the border, in Thailand, not here, in Phnom Penh. They ask him to please pass on their requests, to impress upon someone that there are things they need, now, right away. Persistently, they crowd in on him, but it is as if they are restrained, their limbs move slowly, or is it his eyes that are deceiving him because all he sees are wraiths, bodies out of proportion who, in the morning when he emerges from his cotton sheets, might very well be dead. An old man who speaks English and claims to be the former Minister of Public Works asks him to come back tomorrow and take a letter to his sister, now living in California. He wants to tell her that her children are dead but her husband concealed his identity and lived. The volume of his voice flickers along with the lights in the jars. Hiroji shows the man a photograph of James. The former Minister of Public Works studies his brother's face and then directs him down along the road, to Tun or Old Mak, maybe one of them will know.

"What cooperative?" Tun asks, holding the photo close to his eyes.

Hiroji shakes his head.

"Do you know what district, what sector?"

"He lived in Phnom Penh," Hiroji says.

"*Non, non,*" a woman interjects. "*Personne a habité ici.*"

Two men nearby are screaming at each other. Their fists are out, faces venomous, but people watch languidly. It is simultaneously loud and still and bright and fast. One man picks up a brick, wraps it in his scarf, and begins to swing the weapon, like a cowboy, over his head. Beside Hiroji, the woman says, "*Vas-y.* Get away from here." She is talking to herself, but the French and

Khmer words lodge in his mind. Forcefully, she pushes him back.

He passes through the crowd, disoriented. He is holding James's photograph and an old man selling individual slices of grapefruit runs after him and takes the photo from him.

He tells Hiroji, in graceful English, "I know this man. This is the friend of Dararith. The doctor."

"Yes," Hiroji says, stunned. "The doctor." The crowd is grumbling now, in counterpoint to the yelling. "James Matsui. Sometimes he went by Ichiro or Junichiro."

"But he died," the old man says. "He died and left his wife behind, long before April 17."

"No, that isn't the same person."

"Of course it is," the old man says calmly. "I went to the wedding. Yes, the sister of Dararith."

"Where is Dararith now?"

"Dead."

"And his sister?"

"Oh, certainly dead." The man hands the photograph back to Hiroji, his expression unreadable in the twilight. "She taught my son. She was a good girl, a good teacher."

"It must be a different man."

"On my soul," the old man says, his voice barely audible above the commotion behind them. "Yes. On my soul. Sorya and Dararith lived on Monivong. If you want, I will show you the place."

They walk to Monivong, up and down the wide street, past people so pitiful Hiroji looks past them to the darkened buildings, the smashed windows, and broken-down doors. Campfires burn haltingly. There is rubbish everywhere. The old man moves very slowly, he gets confused and turns around, squints up at the French façades, wonders aloud if the shutters were blue or green. He sighs and says, "My eyesight is very poor now. I believe it was this building but . . . third floor or fifth floor? An odd number. I'm very sorry. It's difficult at night. I can see it in my mind but I don't see it here."

They stand for a few moments gazing up at the shadowed buildings.

"If you remember," Hiroji says at last, "will you come and find me?"

"Of course, of course. I would be happy to."

In neat block letters, Hiroji writes the name of the hotel and then the address of the Red Cross office.

"I'll come speak to you again," he tells the man.

"Of course."

Hiroji buys two whole grapefruit and carries on. More people mumble over the photograph, they ask themselves is this so-and-so, is this the son of our friend Tan? He hears a dozen leads and possibilities, he writes each one down in a black notebook, each one as likely and unlikely as the next.

Night after night, he wanders through Phnom Penh and the wary Vietnamese soldiers leave him alone, the rats scurry from underfoot, children watch him pass as if he were an apparition.

"You're stubborn," his brother says.

"I'm tired, James."

"Do you remember Dad?"

"I'm so tired now."

"It's okay. He didn't want to be remembered. It was war, he said. 'It was just another war.' That's why he did the things he did."

"What kinds of things?"

His brother shakes his head impatiently.

A girl on the street asks him, "Mister, where are you from?"

"Canada."

She looks at him, puzzled. A deep frown spreads across her forehead. "Czechoslovakia," she says suddenly, victoriously.

"Canada," he says.

She smiles and she keeps smiling, her eyes are half-mad and he has to look away.

"Mister," she says slowly. "Do you want to help me?"

He covers his face with his hands.

The thing is, a part of him wants to remain in Phnom Penh. The jungle eats the buildings up, and the people come and push it back, and violence isn't hidden anywhere, it just is what it is, it dogs you like the river, it arrives and returns, it arrives and remains.

He tells James, "I won't abandon you."

"You'll never be ready," his brother says impatiently. "You never had it in you."

The rains start. He's ashamed to witness such hardship. People cling to nothing, they stare out with empty expressions, a blankness that seems like a screwed-on lid, slowly cracking under the pressure. Meanwhile, he goes back, every night, to the Hotel Samaki, where a three-course dinner is served on fragile painted plates. The food in the hotel is fresh and bountiful, the Red Cross has its own private stock of food. He's never eaten so well in his life. The sound of the metal forks raking against the plates disturbs him. He wants to pray or meditate or walk on water. Stories pile up in his black notebook: the Japanese cameraman who was captured in 1973 and killed. The Canadian sailor who washed up on the south coast in 1977, he was imprisoned and finally executed. All the children who, orphaned or separated, flew away to the other side of the world.

At the hotel, he stands, drenched, under the once-sublime balustrade. The water carries lost objects, a rubber sandal, a baby's tub. A boy races to retrieve usable items, the water rising as high as his waist. Thirty years later, Hiroji thinks he sees him again, the very same child, except that this one is shouting, pursued by another boy, and the street is a current of reflected colours, headlights, and neon signs rubbing the darkness. Phnom Penh is under water again, but this time it is strange and out of season. Nuong snaps and unsnaps his cell phone, extends an umbrella, and guides Hiroji through the rivered streets to Nuong's own guesthouse, the Lowell Hotel. A young helper lifts Hiroji's suitcase, frowns, tells Nuong that this Korean tourist has come empty-handed. Hiroji stands like a potted plant, gazing at Nuong's wife, she is fine-boned and lovely, her flower-patterned dress quivering in the fan's current. "A twenty-hour flight!" Nuong is saying. "Just one more set of stairs." They go up and up. Behind them, the helper, Tarek, balances the suitcase on his shoulder. "The best room," he hears, "you can stay as long as you want," and it *is* comfortable, cool and sun-dappled. Nuong aims a remote at the ceiling and the air conditioning clanks into life. "Relax for an hour or so, then we'll go to dinner. The rains will stop. There's a great place . . ." and Hiroji sits on the bed. There is the bodhisattva just as it was, one hand pointing to heaven, the other caressing the earth. "It's yours," Nuong is saying. "Do you remember? You gave it to me at the airport, before I boarded the plane. I've always kept it." When the door closes, Hiroji stands for a long time at the window, trying to understand the choice he's made, the things he's done. There's no going home now. Some part of him is still in the airplane, still looking down, unable to see.

Three weeks went by and he travelled from one edge of the country to the other. Sometimes Nuong accompanied

him, but usually Hiroji went with Tarek. They went by
car or motorbike, they spent days away from Phnom
Penh. First stop, the Dangrek Mountains, Sisophon,
the narrow road to the Thai border. Turning east again,
to Kampong Thom, then crisscrossing southwest. He
thought he could go forever, towns giving way to villages, giving way to lone shacks. Hiroji carried the same
black notebook he had used in 1979. It was the hot
season. Sometimes he and Tarek sat for hours, waiting
for the sun to retreat. Tarek grinned helplessly at the
ladies, they were a pink- or blue- or violet-shirted flock
of swans, arranged on hammocks. Hiroji saw James everywhere, in the old men resting their elbows on plastic
tables, sitting astride their motorbikes. Monks hurried
by, bright along the road like autumn leaves.

When he had been in Cambodia nearly a month,
Nuong introduced him to Bonny. He was a fixer, a sur-
vivor who had made a living digging up the dead. In
the bar where they met, he wore a loud, disco-era shirt,
sunglasses up on his forehead, and a drooping frangipani behind his ear. Men like Bonny, Nuong said, were
Cambodia's secret service. Usually, they were former
Khmer Rouge, disbanded in the mid-1990s when the co-
alition government fell apart, who had since reinvented
themselves as private detectives. They had taken foreign journalists to Pol Pot, to Comrade Duch, and Ta
Mok. "Everyone is my friend," Bonny told him. He had
the most piercing eyes Hiroji had ever seen. "From the

cave-dwellers to the politicians to the CIA. Now you," he said, sliding his mirrored sunglasses down, "you are my friend." Hiroji gazed into the double reflection of himself, the restaurant, the beer girls behind them.

He paid Bonny in American dollars. A few weeks later, at the height of the dry season, the fixer knocked on Hiroji's door.

He entered the room in a calico shirt. In his hand, he brandished a dozen photographs. "Didn't I tell you?" he said, smiling his sunlit smile. "Bonny can work miracles."

He lay the photographs on the bedspread. Hiroji stood and stared. The face in the picture was older, lined, and achingly familiar. He saw his mother's eyes. Bonny was speaking and Hiroji had to shade his face, block the man's grin, in order to comprehend. James was living under a false name, Bonny said. *Kwan*. A decade ago, he had moved to northern Laos, and he lived there with a woman and her grown children. The woman was Laotian but had lived in Cambodia nearly all her life. *Vanna*.

"Look," Bonny said. "I even bought you an airplane ticket. You leave tomorrow for Luang Prabang." He tapped his chest with the open flat of his hand. "Courtesy of Bonny."

Hiroji felt nothing.

This was the initial fist of shock.

"Your brother is alive," Bonny said. Grave, sympathetic.

That night, Hiroji and Nuong went to a bar on the riverside. The walls sang with tropical light. The foreigners were loud and drunk but Hiroji, unbearably sober, remembered his mother who had died two decades ago. He thought of all the ways he had abandoned James little by little, year by year. By the time he moved to Montreal, he had given up returning to the Thai border and to Cambodia. Nuong ordered a round of drinks. Outside, moto drivers slept on the seats of their vehicles, their bare feet balanced on the handlebars. Hiroji drank beer and then whiskey and then beer again. Beside him, the waitress played with the sleeve of her uniform, staring at the clients as if they were images on a television screen. He told Nuong that he was ready to leave his brother behind. "Yes," Nuong said, not meeting his eyes. Why was it that forgetting James was like cutting off his hand, but his brother had chosen to live an entire life away from them? Could they possibly still be brothers? If so, it couldn't mean anything. Tomorrow he would go home to Canada. He would explain his disappearance as a fugue state, an amnesia that carries a person away for weeks, even months. He would return and throw himself into his work, already new ideas and research projects were taking root in his mind. He would accept that he had been the only one looking, it was his own guilt that had driven him here. The whiskey softened his thoughts. He was a good researcher, a good man. He had let his mother down but, still, it was no reason for weeping.

"Come on," Nuong said. "Let's go to the river. Let's get out of here and see the city."

Hiroji arrived in Luang Prabang the next afternoon and hired a driver to take him to James's village. In the road, children came and swirled around him, they called him *farang Hmong*, he gave them candy and they flew off like summer birds. He followed the directions that Bonny had given him. He went up to the house, unsure whether to knock or push the door open, he had the uneasy sensation that it was himself he would see, as if all the lying and forging of documents had finally caught up to him. He knocked and eventually an old man opened the door, an old man who looked just like the photographs of their father, a father Hiroji could barely recall.

"James," he said.

The man didn't respond.

"I was told that you were here."

The man stared past him.

"It's me, Hiroji."

He could hear children everywhere, he could hear water boiling, strangely near, persistent voices, it must be the neighbour's, a door smacking closed, chickens. "Can I come in?" he asked. "Just for a few minutes."

James pulled the door open a little wider and stepped back. It was cool inside, away from the glare of the sun.

His brother made him tea.

Hiroji said, "I'm a doctor now. I live in Montreal."

His brother was barely listening. He moved constantly, sipping tea, eating peanuts, standing up to wipe the table, getting ice for the beer, cleaning glasses, misting a baby plant, adjusting the volume of the radio, up, down, lower, then finally moving the radio to a different room entirely without ever switching it off. A woman came out of the room. She was bare foot, wearing a blouse and a blue *sampot*. When she saw Hiroji, she smiled at him, her eyebrows lifting in a question. James spoke to her in a language he didn't understand. A few minutes later, the woman, perhaps in her mid-fifties, with a dignified, gracious face, slid her feet into a pair of sandals and left the house.

Hiroji opened his bag and took out an envelope. He removed photocopies of the letters that James had sent to him before he disappeared, a photograph of their family, of his mother's funeral, of their childhood home in Vancouver. A photograph of James as a child.

James studied them from afar. Then he stood up, set more beer on the table, went into another room, and shut the door behind him.

Hiroji shifted his weight on the flimsy chair. It was okay, he thought. How could you prove to someone that you knew them? How could you prove that you were related by blood and something more than blood? It felt useless. So innate as to be useless. He could leave now.

This room would still exist, his brother would still be here, but the cut glass inside himself would no longer pain him. It was finished. Wasn't that good enough?

He got up and knocked on the closed door.

"Ichiro," he said. "Don't you know who I am?"

"Don't be upset," his brother said. His voice was muffled. "It's no use being upset. What's done is done."

Something, bitterness or grief, was choking him but nothing came out, no blame, no words. He stood up to leave. When he opened the door, the warm air soothed him, but there were people outside enjoying the evening, there were children beside two oxen, and a girl in a wheelchair with her father behind her. They seemed like impossible obstacles so he went back inside. A little girl followed him through the door. James had emerged, he had already started to clear the table, and the little girl went to James and held his hand.

Hiroji walked past them, to the back of the house. He climbed a staircase and found himself on a sheltered veranda, with a view of the jungle. He felt that he was absurd and out of proportion and his hands were too big for his arms, his neck was too long, his head too heavy. He sat down on the veranda. An ant sidled up his foot and he brushed it lightly away. When he lay back, it was as if he was setting his exhaustion, an infinite misunderstanding, against the floor.

Much later, footsteps sounded. His brother stood over him.

"When did she die?" his brother said, holding a picture of their mother.

"A few years after we lost you. She died of cancer."

His brother nodded, still staring at the photo. Hiroji was too tired to sit up. He closed his eyes.

"I used to tell myself," James said, "that my family was living in California, that I should try to reach them. So many children went to America. But how could I get there? I tried to go but . . . it was difficult. I was afraid."

Hiroji looked up. "We lived in Vancouver. Don't you remember? Is that why you never came back?"

"No," James said. "My family."

Hiroji said nothing.

"Dararith, my baby boy. My sweet boy. I waited for him, but he never came. I looked everywhere but he couldn't be found." He shook his head. "I had to stop searching. In the end, I had to give him up."

There was a closed room behind Hiroji. James went inside and returned with a full bottle and two dusty glasses. When Hiroji drank the liquor, it burned everything on its cascade down and made the trees spin silently. He emptied the glass quickly, and so did James. His brother poured generously. The stars glistened. On the road outside, Hiroji thought he saw his mother. She was walking through the village. She had come to fetch her coat, and now she wrapped it tight around herself. She told him not to follow her. He felt lost, immaterial.

He wanted to shelter the things he loved, to keep them from washing away.

"Say goodbye," his mother said.

He was running in place, he was afraid to drown, he was afraid to touch land.

"Isn't this what you wanted?" She looked at him with such intensity, such understanding. "You've already come so far. Hold your brother and say goodbye."

She did up the buttons on her coat and turned away.

[end]

Hiroji travels with me, back through the mountains, eleven hours in a bus with a rattling air conditioner, all the way to the airport in Vientiane. After I fly home to Canada, he'll go north again, to James. We talk about the BRC, about my family, about the things that have changed and not changed since Hiroji went away. Together, we ascend through limestone valleys, we shoulder along hairpin turns. Exhausted vehicles wait in the shade, doors flung open at the side of the highway.

At a rest stop in the mountains, I call Navin. "Where are you?" he asks and I try to find words to describe this place, ivory sky, stilt houses, and children everywhere. A little boy named Pomme is leaning against Hiroji's legs, watching his mother, who sells mangosteens to the passing travellers. The boy calls us *farang Hmong*,

Westerners with a face like his, strangers both foreign and familiar.

Kiri comes on the line. He says that he is in my old bed, in Lena's house. He asks me if I still remember it and I say, Yes, I remember.

"We went to the cemetery," he says. "We put flowers there, for Lena. Lilies."

The air up here, in the high altitudes, is thin, cooling. Hiroji is kneeling on the ground, talking to the boy, who stares shyly up at the tall trees.

"Dad told me, sometimes when you miss somebody, you lose yourself for a little while." Between our voices, static, continents. "Promise me," my son says. "Don't disappear."

Between us, cascading mountains, an infinite vista. I make this promise.

In the bus, Hiroji drifts to sleep, his head cushioned by a rolled-up coat. A family across the aisle from us brings out green desserts and the children eat them blissfully. The father sleeps and his wife watches him, her face lined with anxiety and I remember how, long ago, my parents' lives came apart. One night, Sopham woke from a nightmare and my mother climbed into bed with us. My father came and lit a cigarette and the tiny orange glow held all my attention, burning slowly out. They did not speak to each other. I yearned for their argument to spill over, to explode, to end. One day I came home from school and I saw my father leaning against the kitchen wall, my mother seated at the table, weeping. I heard her accuse him, and my father said nothing. My mother's face could not be borne. I wanted to go to them, to help them somehow, but it was not possible.

My childhood is full of images like this, passing moments I didn't understand, as if I were looking through a window into the aftermath of a great event. The school year passed and another began. Sopham and I grew accustomed to our parents' silence, to the way they withdrew from each other. And then, one night, I saw them sitting side by side, their shoulders touching. Later on, I saw my father caress my mother's face and between them, once more, was a world I couldn't enter, full of pathos and history and seeking. What I saw this time was not an aftermath, but a window open to a different way of loving each other. My mother's longing for my father returns to me. At the end, their lives had grown so intertwined the one could not go on, could not survive, without the other. I had known this from the beginning, from the moment when my father was taken away. From that loss, there had been no return. I try to face the depth of her love. The way she never abandoned us, and how it tore her open.

I want to remember the way they lived, carried forward by intimacies and dreams I cannot know. The way they lived much more than the remaining days could give them.

The bus goes on, past cerulean lakes and ragged caves, past mist encroaching on the jungle.

Hiroji wakes. He takes his jacket and lays it across his knees. "I was trying to remember my brother's face," he says. "Before he left for the east, when we were young. But, somehow, that memory of him has gone away." How many lives can we live? I wonder. How many can we steal back and piece together? I cannot measure how much Hiroji and James have given me, in trust, in friendship.

I remember the stories my mother used to tell me, stories that had been handed down by her own grand-mother's grandmother, who had married a merchant and travelled from the villages outside of Battambang. My mother once told me that when a child is born, threads are tied around the infant's wrists to bind her soul to her body. The soul is a slippery thing. A door slammed too loudly can send it running. A beautiful, shining object can catch its attention and lure it away. But in darkness, unpursued, the soul, the *pralung*, can climb back in through an open window, it can be returned to you. We did not come in solitude, my mother told me. Inside us, from the begin-ning, we were entrusted with many lives. From the first morning to the last, we try to carry them until the end.

"When everything is finished here, will you come home?" I ask Hiroji.

The passing landscape, the folding light, reflects in his eyes. He turns to look at me. "Yes," he says. "I will."

I imagine awaiting his arrival, remembering my own. The sky is such a pure and fragile white, filling all the space between the trees and the road.

Keep in touch with
Granta Books:

Visit grantabooks.com to discover more.

GRANTA

Also by Madeleine Thien and available from Granta Books
www.grantabooks.com

CERTAINTY

'A nuanced study of love, displacement and the quicksilver
nature of certitude . . . [which] gleams with emotional
clarity' *Observer*

Gail Lim is haunted by the mysterious events of her
father's childhood in war-torn Asia. As a boy, Matthew
Lim hid in the jungle in Japanese-occupied Sandakan,
British North Borneo, with Ani, a girl whose friendship
shaped the rest of his life. Together they barely survive
the terrifying events of the war which ultimately splits
them apart – until, years later, they meet again, only to
endure another separation. Crossing continents, cultures
and time, *Certainty* explores the legacies of loss, the
dislocations of war and the redemptive qualities of love.

'Compelling and thoughtful . . . Thien has a gift for
beautifully shaped images that she uses to powerful effect'
Independent

'Finely crafted, moving, and weighty, *Certainty* is one of those
rare novels that combines intimacy with an elusive sense of
the epic' Tash Aw

'Elegant writing . . . [which explores] the idea and purpose of
memory and its propulsive effect . . . as if layers of the past
have been draped over the present and over each other' *TLS*

'An important and compelling writer' *Guardian*

Also by Madeleine Thien and available from Granta Books
www.grantabooks.com

DO NOT SAY WE HAVE NOTHING

Shortlisted for the Man Booker Prize 2016

Winner of the Scotiabank Giller Prize 2016

Winner of the Governor General's Literary Award 2016

In 1990, ten-year-old Marie and her mother take in a young
woman fleeing the aftermath of the Tiananmen Square
protests. Her name is Ai-ming. She brings stories of her
family under Chairman Mao, and of revolutionary idealism,
music and silence, which span the course of China's recent
turbulent history, and have deep and lasting consequences
for Ai-ming – and for Marie.

'Epic in scope and delicate in detail' *Sunday Times*
'Best Books of the Year'

'A vivid, magisterial novel . . . A moving and extraordinary
evocation of the 20th-century tragedy of China . . . [from]
an important and compelling writer' Isabel Hilton, *Guardian*

'A piercing blur of fiction and history' *Spectator*

'Enchanting . . . reminds us what fiction can do'
New Statesman

'Deeply moving . . . full of wisdom, comedy and beauty'
Herald

'Courageous and profound' *Observer*